If Hannah wasn't mistaken…

Daniel Raber was a bit of a charmer. She would do well to keep things strictly to necessity.

"You can use the phone and M.J. can entertain the men with stories about rock skipping and milk cows." Daniel moved through the doorway and turned back to her.

"I don't think that is a good idea, Daniel. Bryan said stay out of sight as much as possible. The fewer people we meet, the better."

"I think it's a fine idea. So bring me lunch tomorrow, use the phone and let me show off those pretty girls." He moved down the hall before she could even object. He'd said that as if he wanted to parade her children around as his own. Part of her took offense, as they were not his children, but Hannah couldn't help another part of herself, the fanciful part she rarely let out of its box. What would be the benefits of a father figure like Daniel? She shook the thought off quickly.

They weren't his, and neither was she.

Raised in Kentucky timber country, **Mindy Steele** has been writing since she could hold a crayon against the wall. Inspired by her rural surroundings, she writes Amish romance peppered with the right amount of charms for all the senses to make you laugh, cry, hold your breath and root for the happy-ever-after ending. A mother of four, Mindy enjoys coffee indulgences, weekend road trips and researching her next book.

Books by Mindy Steele

Love Inspired

His Amish Wife's Hidden Past

Visit the Author Profile page at Harlequin.com.

His Amish Wife's Hidden Past

Mindy Steele

LOVE INSPIRED
INSPIRATIONAL ROMANCE

LOVE INSPIRED®
INSPIRATIONAL ROMANCE

Recycling programs
for this product may
not exist in your area.

ISBN-13: 978-1-335-56725-3

His Amish Wife's Hidden Past

Copyright © 2021 by Mindy Steele

This edition published by arrangement with Harlequin Books S.A.

For questions and comments about the quality of this book, please contact us at CustomerService@Harlequin.com.

Love Inspired
22 Adelaide St. West, 40th Floor
Toronto, Ontario M5H 4E3, Canada
www.Harlequin.com

Printed in U.S.A.

In the fear of the Lord is strong confidence:
and his children shall have a place of refuge.
—*Proverbs* 14:26

To Julie and Connie

Thank you.

Chapter One

Daniel Raber stood on his mill office porch, watching his two hired mill hands amble toward their buggies. Another long day was over and Daniel was glad to see it go. Even he was feeling the effects of rushing to finish another lumber order in his tired bones.

September had started out humid and full of misery, but today, as ashen clouds moved gradually overhead, he felt the change of the seasons ignite. A slight chill of a rare northern wind blew over the Kentucky dirt. He looped both thumbs into his suspenders, closed his eyes, and inhaled the cool whiff mingled with sawdust and dusty earth. Life was shifting again. Imbalance was absolute.

Opening his eyes, he shoved the inkling aside. He had long broken away from trusting his gut, accepting *Gott*'s will in his daily life, but even in trusting *Gott*, one couldn't ignore awareness.

Slapping his dusty straw hat against his britches leg, he headed for the house. It was a mere stroll away over one slight rise in an earth dressed in pastured grasses where his horses and a few lowly cattle grazed. He had a lot to be thankful for. A successful milling business, a comfy home and all the things one needed for a peaceful, content life. So why today was he feeling off-kilter? He had long been cured of his bouts of melancholy, and learned to never look back, just forward.

Late-afternoon skies threatened rain above, but Daniel doubted they would make good on it. He finished milking, managed to wrangle four pesky goats back into their fences and put together a nice meal for one before the first stars winked. He was used to solitude within the quiet two-story home, but there were days when he missed companionship, the sense of family. He had his community, and it was enough, mostly, but occasionally when the rains lingered too long or the nights were simply cold and dreary, that loneliness snagged hold and left him wanting.

He was thirty-six, too old to be a bachelor, too young to start courting again. However, a family seemed to be niggling his thoughts of late. No one had caught his attention, not even Margaret Sayer, who made a habit of visiting every Tuesday with a new dish for him to sample. It was selfish, he thought, daring to ask *Gott* for more after He directed Daniel home and blessed him with so much already.

He turned off the gas burner and removed the pan of boiled potatoes from the stove. He sprinkled a dash of salt and set them by his plate before fetching the leftover chicken from the oven. It was a good thing he had tried his hand at cooking growing up when *Mudder* encouraged it. *A man who can cook will never go hungry, Mudder* had said. He poured himself a glass of water and took his seat at the head of the table.

The dim room grew dimmer, eerily so. Maybe that storm was going to hit Miller's Creek after all. Daniel lowered his head to pray for the void in his life to be filled, ignoring the first pings on the porch roof. His animals were safe and secure in the barn, his business, the same, and the house had proven years ago when a tornado blew near that it could withstand a mighty storm sure enough. So why did he feel unsettled? He only got that gut-jerk feeling when something bad was about to happen. So he prayed for strength.

Halfway into his supper, a hard knock came

at the door. He pushed back his chair and went to answer. The wind outside howled, the rain gaining momentum, making a racket against the tin roofs of the porch, barn and outbuildings. He opened the door and found himself looking down at his uncle, the bishop.

"Joshua." Daniel quickly stepped back at the sight of the drenched willowy man and let him hurry inside. "What brings you out in this?" Another shadow followed. Under his dripping, more-sleek version of rain gear, Daniel noted the suit. The stranger wasn't Amish, but the dark foyer gave little help on his identity.

"Evening, Daniel," the bishop greeted in his oddly deep voice for such a small frame. His long beard glistened against the light from the lamps burning in the next room, revealing a healthy dose of silver woven into dark coarse hairs. "This is Bryan Bates. He is a government agent." Daniel's forehead lifted in surprise. "He asked that he may speak with you," Joshua added, removing his black felt hat and shedding his raincoat, comfortably hanging them on an empty wooden wall peg nearby. Though *ferhoodled*, Daniel ushered both men into the kitchen where the gas lanterns burned brightest.

"Let me put on the kettle," Daniel said. He hated that his instincts were so keen. Both his *onkel* and the agent took a seat. *"Was ist letz?"* Daniel asked his *onkel*, but only received a sorrowful expression in reply. Joshua wasn't a man of limited words, ever. Daniel turned to the pudgy agent with shoes shinier than the blackest onyx littering the creek beds out back.

"Well, I'm actually a US marshal," Bates replied as he took in the room, a simple home free of adornments with more dust than Daniel could tackle daily given his business and farm duties. "It seems we have disrupted your supper." Before Daniel could offer either man a plate—he always made more than he needed—Joshua spoke again.

"The marshal," his uncle corrected, "has news to share with you." He stood and joined Daniel at the stove. Another sign something bad was coming. "I think you should sit down. I'll tend to making *kaffi*." Daniel found nothing in that solemn expression.

"Are you here as my bishop, or my *onkel*?" Daniel had no immediate family aside from Joshua, his business followed all the English-made mandates and not one horse had ever escaped the field. And if one of those pesky goats Caleb Byler tricked him into taking on had gotten out and caused an accident on the main road, well, the county deputy would be the one sitting in his kitchen right now, not a US marshal.

"Please, Mr. Raber, have a seat." It was an order, the way he said it, but Daniel detected a hint of pity in it. "You have been a hard man to find." The marshal pinned him with a probing gaze. Daniel sat in the nearest chair, always one to obey authority, unlike his *bruder* who'd had a habit of headbutting it.

"This is nice country you got out here. Not many neighbors. Quiet," Bates assessed as Joshua poured three cups of *kaffi* and brought them to the table. His northern accent only added to the mystery of his presence. "Have you lived here long?" Bates asked, taking a sip of the stout brew without so much as pruning his features. His *onkel* was known for his kind outreach to others, his penchant for hard candy, and his powerful *kaffi*.

"It was my family's homestead, and *jah*, going on eleven years now. You should say what you came to say. I'm not one who likes dragging a thing out if it can be helped." Daniel crossed both arms across his chest, ignoring the look of amusement smeared on the marshal's face.

"Then I will get straight to it. I'm from Indiana, where we have been investigating a homicide," Marshal Bates said. "The killer shot a detective after he and another man broke into his home. Tell me, Mr. Raber, do you know a Micah Reynolds?"

"*Nee*, I do not, nor have I ever lived in Indiana." Daniel remained calm though his confusion was building.

"Micah was a close friend of mine, a detective for about eight years. He was working on a case involving stolen firearms and other undesirable things. We suspect he got too close and Marotta, a very bad and wealthy man, wanted to see that Micah didn't get any closer." The marshal lowered his head and stared into his cup.

"I'm sorry about your friend, but I still don't know why you're telling me any of this or why you brought my bishop out in this weather to do it," Daniel said.

"Micah Reynolds wasn't my friend's birth name. It took some digging but I found out his real name was Michael Raber." The news slammed like a hammer into Daniel's chest. The sudden shock to his system felt like a streak of lightning had made its way in and found him, on purpose.

His brother was dead?

"Michael? Are you sure?"

"Yes, Mr. Raber. I'm sorry, but yes. Michael Raber was murdered on Tuesday in his home by a man named Nicholas Corsetti." Thunder crashed outside matching Daniel's rumbling emotions.

Daniel got to his feet and went to the sink. "He's dead. My *bruder* is dead," he muttered, staring out into the storm that found him living peacefully here in his birthplace. He gripped the sink to keep his hands from shaking. Part of him always expected Michael to succumb to his bad habits or shady friends, but the news still made a dent in Daniel's heart.

"*Kumm*, Daniel. There is more to discuss and many decisions to be made this night," Joshua urged. Daniel didn't want to hear more.

He hated tears. Not for their weakness, but for what they represented. He let a couple freefall without caring either way. His brother was dead. Now he truly was alone in the world.

As the marshal continued, Daniel leaned forward and tried to absorb everything he was saying, but he was going to be sick. His brother had a family, three children, and one had witnessed the unimaginable. Daniel worked through his own emotional battle and grasped the severity of what the marshal was saying. Michael's family was in danger. "We can't let anything happen to them," he muttered.

"Glad we can agree." Both men locked gazes. Daniel understood the family, *his* family, needed a place to hide until a killer could be found. One didn't need to be a smart man to predict what came next. Straightening, Daniel braced himself for it.

"They want to hide them here," Joshua put in.

"No one would think to look in Amish country for them," the marshal said sweeping an arm over the room. "It's perfect."

"And yet, you found me." It was a stupid idea, and one that might get Michael's family killed. Amish didn't believe in confrontation. Surely the marshal wasn't thinking clearly.

"I found you because of an old photo your brother carried." The marshal pulled a photograph from his coat pocket and slid it across the table. Daniel gingerly lifted it and stared into the past, the family they once were smiling back at him. The outside world had taken them all and now that outside world was here, knocking on his door.

"Do they know Michael was Amish? That he had a *bruder*?" Daniel ran his thumb over the images of his family and tried wrapping his head around the situation.

"No, and they don't need to until after this is all over. I insist on that part. She has been hit with a lot in a short time. I don't want to overwhelm her with more." Daniel understood that well enough. For as heavy as his heart was feeling right now, Michael's wife was surely burdened with more.

"I will help any way I can for my *bruder*'s family, but I'm not sure how to hide a woman and three *kinner* here. Amish do things differently. Men and women don't simply live under the same roof unless they're…" Joshua touched his shoulder and squeezed. Daniel got to his feet again. "I can't marry my *bruder*'s wife, an *Englischer*."

"So you have another interest then," his *onkel* challenged.

"You know I do not," Daniel shot back. "And this is not the time for you to be addressing my single status, *Onkel*." Daniel narrowed his look. Joshua ran his boney finger over his *kaffi* cup and grinned. *So he is using this horrible ordeal to marry me off.* Daniel groaned to himself.

"You have a responsibility. She is a widow with three *kinner* and needs a husband, a protector and a provider. Many in our community marry for far less."

"They need someone who knows the outside world enough to help them fit in to this one." The marshal continued to persuade him. Daniel let out a slow breath as the reality sank in. A loveless marriage to a woman of his brother's choosing and three kids. "I'll give you two a minute to talk this through. I need to radio in and have the family brought on over." The marshal moved toward the door and pulled his phone from his jacket pocket.

"Here! Tonight?" Daniel called after him.

"I know this is a lot, so take that minute I mentioned to absorb everything I have told you, because that's what Magnolia is doing right now as she is being briefed about what she must do for her children's safety. I understand the commitment here, the sacrifice. But you aren't the only one making them. They need you." How could Daniel refuse now?

Appetite gone, Daniel began clearing the table. There were no instructions on how to handle a matter such as this, and if there had been, he would have never thought to read them.

He poured Joshua's bitter brew down the sink and started a fresh pot to percolate on the back burner. This night was certainly going to require it.

Thiry-year-old Magnolia Reynolds swiped the rain from her face and stepped into the dimly lit house behind the US marshal. Three days ago she was complaining about real estate contracts and how her husband breaking another promise to their children meant she would spend a night camping in the backyard while September gnats ate away at her flesh. Now, as a storm barreled overhead, she found herself widowed and running for her life.

She pulled Roslyn closer against her side as Sadie, her youngest, clung to her neck like a life raft. With all the emotions swirling inside her, she couldn't imagine what waves of confusion her daughters were feeling, but fear was certainly high on the list.

And now she was expected to put their lives in the hands of strangers. It was ironic, seeing as she had married a man who had built his fortune on lies and broken promises. A man who left her alone to face the consequences of his actions.

No matter the mixture of anger and fear, her heart was shattered. Micah was gone, her children traumatized, and Roslyn—at only six years of age—was a possible target for a madman. She accepted witness protection, trusting the marshal's concerns held value, but how was their best option for hiding marrying a stranger and pretending to be something she was not? Being tossed about most of her life had prepared her for many things, but this time, Magnolia feared she might not adapt, or blend in, so easily.

Marshal Bates, a longtime family friend, led the way inside the large house and she and her children cautiously followed, flanked by the two agents assigned to them. Agent Lawson was brawny and quiet, just as one might picture secret agents to be. Agent Moore, a female version of protection, was petite and far less serious. She made certain Magnolia understood what was expected of her to keep her daughters safe. Agent Moore urged her forward, just as she had done from the moment Magnolia's life had spun out of control.

"I want to go home. It's not fair," her eldest, Jasmine, protested as they moved into a large open kitchen. *It wasn't fair*, but what choice did they have?

Her gaze lifted immediately to the stranger as he turned from the stove and locked eyes with her. He was tall, with a dark stare and surprisingly was not as she pictured at all. Agent Moore had explained the common Amish dress, the stern nature, conformity, and devout faith they presented. He looked nothing of the sort. He had no beard or scowl and didn't look much older than her. If not for the suspenders and hair much too long to be considered appropriate, he looked like any man on the street back home in Indiana.

His gaze made a quick study of them and

she clutched her children protectively closer, careful not to tug on Roslyn's long, dark braid as she did. She might not have many choices right now, but she wasn't about to hand out her trust too swiftly.

Her youngest two daughters were still dressed in matching pink pajamas. Roslyn had her favorite purple shoes, but no socks. If only she'd had more time to pack before the marshals swept them away from their lives only to drop them into a world completely foreign to her.

Jasmine gave her that signature sulk. They shared the same blonde hair and blue eyes, but Jasmine had also inherited her father's long legs and short temper. Magnolia passed her a begging glance to try harder and accept what was taking place. She had explained they would now live here, pretend to be other people, until life was safe again. Her daughters understood mostly what was necessary for their survival right now.

Turning her attention back to the stranger again, she wondered what was going through his thoughts, and what kind of man who looked like this one wasn't already married but agreeing to put his life at risk for strangers. She tried not to appear too fragile, but the last few days had taken a lot out of her.

In jeans and a plain rose-colored button-up shirt she looked far from a perfectly Plain woman. Her flip-flops revealed red painted toenails that matched her fingertips. She didn't look showy or arrogant, absent from her normal attire, but under his scrutiny, she knew she didn't look like a potential Amish bride either. It was her lot in life, seldom fitting in anywhere. She would deal with this as she did everything life tossed at her. By the skin of her teeth.

In his narrowed gaze, her chin lifted slightly, defining her willingness to do what she had to, marry a stranger, no matter how she wished not to. When he offered a curt nod, Magnolia accepted it as a silent agreement that he too would do what he had to do. Exhaustion was clearly navigating her steps at this point. But for the first time in three days, her shoulders relaxed a little.

"Mags, this is Daniel Raber. Daniel, this is Magnolia Reynolds and her daughters, Jasmine, Roslyn and Sadie." She swallowed the lump in her dry throat as Marshal Bates introduced them. Indecision and panic swept through her but she feared speaking out now might be a mistake. The only way to steel her emotions was to focus on their troubles, not her unhinged world.

"Welcome to my home. It is very nice to meet each of you," the stranger welcomed in a low, but friendly, voice.

Sadie lifted her head at the sound of him and studied Daniel closely. Her unruly blonde curls bounced with the tilt of her head. Upon her youngest's request, Magnolia put Sadie down to stand on her own two feet. Her arms were immediately grateful for the rest. The room fell silent as first impressions ran between strangers.

Sadie's big brown eyes took Daniel in, seeing what to make of a man dressed in Amish garb. Then she took three cautious steps forward and held out her hand. Magnolia started to reach out to stop her, but fatigue was making her unsteady. Her youngest had never met a stranger. To Magnolia's surprise Daniel bent eye level to Sadie, and smiled.

"Nice to meet you too. I'm five. Mommy says we have to live here now." Magnolia steeled a breath when Daniel looked to her again. Permission perhaps. When she gave it, his lips tugged to one corner and she knew. Sadie had a way about her to melt most hearts. When Daniel accepted her hand, it felt as if the deal had been made. If he had second thoughts about helping them, he didn't any longer. "I like your house, but…?" Sadie leaned closer and whispered loudly. "I don't like the dark."

"I can add more lamps to help with that." Daniel winked, making her giggle. "But don't be afraid of the dark, little one." He tapped her little button nose.

"At least he likes kids," Agent Moore whispered beside her. For that, Magnolia was thankful.

"But it's the dark." Sadie cocked her head adorably and said in a comical cuteness that had the whole room smiling, "All kinds of things are in the dark."

"*Jah*, but if you can't see anything, what is there to be afraid of?"

She touched her finger to her chin as she was prone to do when contemplating. If Magnolia wasn't mistaken, the tall dark stranger was melting under her daughter's innocent charms. A fleeting thought pronounced itself right then. What kind of man who melted in little girls' smiles would protect them? "Just because I can't see the bad things hiding, don't mean they aren't there."

"*Jah*, true." Daniel matched her finger-to-the-chin gesture. "But just because you can't see *gut* things watching over us, does not mean they aren't there either." Sadie clearly didn't understand, but as always, she smiled anyway.

It took so little effort to warrant a smile from that one. "We will just add more light for now, until you can trust me that there is nothing in the dark here to fear."

"You talk funny," she added. "I like it." Chuckles flowed around them.

"I like the way you talk too." Daniel patted her head and stood. His eyes locked with Magnolia's. Though she would remain guarded, respectfully so, she felt that living here for a time might not be so terrible after all.

Marshal Bates chimed in. "We have new identities for each of you like we talked about earlier. You both should help the girls try to remember them so they don't slip. I would suggest as few outings as possible and keep a low profile, even here." Daniel shot a glance at an older man standing to the shadows. Magnolia hadn't even considered his quiet presence until now. He must be the bishop that Agent Moore spoke of, the one who would marry them, until this nightmare ended.

"Being Amish does not mean one can hide away in solitude." The bishop stepped forward. "Plain life is much the opposite. Our communities thrive on connecting, gathering with family and neighbors regularly. It is the heart of our existence."

"As long as you all understand the limitations," the marshal added in. "The less they are seen, the better." Bates offered the manila folder to Magnolia. Still pondering over what community gatherings included, she ignored him. There was still time to back out and change her mind, wasn't there?

She felt a surge of lightheadedness. She had been living on coffee and prayers up to this point and now exhaustion was taking its full toll on her.

In her hesitation, Daniel stepped forward, accepting the envelope that contained their temporary identities.

"I hope I get a pretty name like Princess Sophia," Sadie said giddily.

"I don't need a new name. You can't just go changing my name," Jasmine protested, and added a foot stomp, punctuating it. With a fresh headache tempting and Jasmine putting up a fuss, Magnolia couldn't think clearly. It was times like these she simply had to accept surrender, let God take control. She was certainly in no frame of mind to take the wheel.

"We will do what is necessary. This isn't about what we want anymore, but what must be done for your safety," Magnolia reminded her eldest as Agent Moore's hand steadied her elbow. Sometimes life simply wasn't fair.

Daniel opened the envelope and pulled out

its contents. "That's your marriage license to keep things official," Bates chimed in. Without changing his blank expression, Daniel tucked the long sheet behind the following pages before looking to her again.

"You are now Hannah." She was glad the agent was keeping her upright as Roslyn shifted from clutching her right leg to gripping her left. He turned to Jasmine's pouting face. She opened her mouth to protest, but quickly drew it shut again. "You are now Catherine Faith." As their former lives began to be stripped away, thunder outside cracked.

Daniel took a few steps closer. This close up he seemed taller and larger than at a distance. He also smelled faintly of sawdust and a summer rain. It was a surprisingly pleasant combination.

"Shall I continue or do you need a moment?" His sincerity shocked her.

She didn't need a moment, she needed to curl into the nearest corner and cry. "Please, continue." He lowered on one knee, bringing him eye level with Roslyn, still clinging to her leg.

"Rosemary. Now that is a beautiful name." Roslyn didn't dare smile or comment, but her fingers loosened slightly from the denim. For the last three days her daughter hadn't spoken a word and Magnolia feared no matter what others said, it would be a long time before she would again. One didn't see death so close and simply forget it. Daniel's brows gathered, detecting the difference in her middle daughter aside from the other two. How much had the marshal shared with him? Bryan insisted Daniel didn't need to know about Micah's dark dealings, only that she and her children needed shelter and safety, and she for one wasn't about to tell him about the man she had married or what he had done to land them here. But it was clear he knew Roslyn had been the one who had seen her father murdered.

"My turn. Sadie Reynolds is hard to spell." Daniel pulled his attentions from Roslyn to her little curly-haired wonder centering the room.

"I agree." When he pulled the next sheet of paper with attached social security card forward, Magnolia noted the pause, the sudden flicker of recognition. He glanced at the bishop lingering in the shadows, clearly distraught and then quickly reined it back in. "How about Martha Jane?" Perhaps he knew another by the common name.

"Martha is pretty and starts with *M*. Mommy taught me all my letters. Jane is *J*. So, M.J." Her brown eyes twinkled. "I like it!" Apparently Daniel did too by the way his dark eyes lit up.

Feeling her legs grow more unsteady, Magnolia quickly put in, "Thank you for agreeing to let us stay here, but it's been a long day. If you could show us which room is ours, I would like to get the girls cleaned up and settled down for bed before we finish what is necessary down here."

Daniel swallowed hard, obviously not in any hurry to finish the duty expected of them. She couldn't blame him but she needed this day over before she collapsed.

"I have rooms for each of them, but I wasn't prepared for..." *Visitors* was too careless a word. "I haven't readied them."

"That won't be necessary, Mr. Raber. We will stay together in one bedroom." She clutched Rosemary closer to her hip. His jaw tightened before he turned to lead the way. Did he already hate this arrangement as much as she did? *Keep on keeping on*, words once gifted her that always helped her remember to keep putting one foot in front of the other no matter the path ahead.

So that's what she did.

Chapter Two

Somewhere in the morning hours, Magnolia had succumbed to exhaustion and slipped off to sleep. Now, she knew she needed to get up, face whatever obstacles another day poured onto her, but she had never felt so tired, so greedy to pull the covers up over her head and waste daylight hours. She reached out an arm and found the sheets cool to the touch. It was only then she realized she wasn't surrounded by little warm bodies. Bolting upright, she found herself disoriented. She wasn't dreaming. These last three days were very real.

Bright morning light filtered through a sheer curtain, revealing a very large and very empty room. A queen-size bed, a small wooden side table and miles of pecan-colored hardwood flooring. Adrenaline seized her and she jumped to her feet and ran out the bedroom door. In the long dim hallway, she tried to collect her bearings, felt her heart begin to gallop. Giggling rose up the stairs, penetrating the rooms in a surprisingly joyous sound. She took a shuddering breath, threw a hand over her racing heart. Giggles were good, very good. After what they had endured the last three days, giggles were a blessing. Emotionally overstrained, she nearly burst into tears at the sounds of laughter. "Thank you, Lord, for landing us someplace safe," she whispered.

Then reality hit her and safe seemed something one shouldn't throw quick trust at. Everything from last night came in a flood. The storm that announced their coming, the Amish house the US Marshals promised would be a safe haven for her daughters and that hurried wedding to a dark stranger to secure that measure of safety. Now her head was spinning again. Hannah gripped the banister with one hand, fisted her stomach with her other and began taking deep breaths.

There was no turning back and changing her mind now. The wheels were in motion and she couldn't stop them even if she wanted to. She had agreed to live with a stranger in his house. It was for them, she reminded herself as her stomach rolled with angst. She needed to be strong, adaptable, and yet the thought of crying for days seemed right too.

"You three enjoy your eggs and pancakes while I run this upstairs," the man, Daniel, spoke below. Could she trust this man? Putting their lives in another's hands was going to take some work. But what other choice did she have? This place, that man, was her safest choice.

Footfalls crossed old wooden floors. The tall figure with midnight black hair climbed the steps, a tray of food in his hands. He looked nothing like a man who served, or cooked. He was all brawn and simple, except for that first impression when he seemed to understand her plight, smiled kindly at her daughters. But how could he understand any of this?

"Gut morgen," he greeted before looking up, knowing she was there. Magnolia blinked as he drew closer and taller in the vanishing distance. Then again, neither of them looked at each other once during the whole stupid charade she was too numb to recall in detail.

"You should eat something," he said, coming to a stop at the top of the landing. His eyes settled on her, sympathy in sorrowful hazel eyes. She couldn't muster a reply, her mind still adrift. She owed him plenty considering he was allowing them to stay here, but what could she say right now? In her silence, he brushed past her and aimed for the shared bedroom.

The scent of warm bacon, something she had sworn off after birthing Roslyn, caused her stomach to gurgle. Daniel pushed back a thin white curtain, letting more of the outside light in.

"Thank you for feeding my children. I never sleep this late." He turned to face her, and she felt her legs grow unsteady. In full light without the play of shadows and a brain too rattled to function, his sturdy frame and handsome looks held her at full attention now. Those few curious glances from last night hadn't given her such a clear view. His tanned face said he was a man who worked outdoors, though she scarcely recalled Bryan mentioning something about him working with wood. He was at least six foot and built like a lumberjack, long legs under dark, broad fall pants, and with shoulders that suggested he could carry some weight without complaint. His light blue shirt had no buttons, no collar. Magnolia hadn't seen a man in suspenders since her second foster home, and Daniel looked nothing like sweet old Henry Clayborn. Hazel eyes, a mossy green with rich earthy tones blended in perfectly. His jaw clenched, noting her dissecting of him. He tilted his head slightly, revealing a slight mark, a scar along his neck. The small trail of raised flesh long healed but present.

"You needed the rest." He lifted a curious brow, eyeing her copiously in return. She still wore the clothes she had arrived in last night and knew her hair required a proper washing or at least a brush. Without the use of her iron, the blond strands tended to wave and stray in various directions. It took ample amounts of product to tame the frizziness. She was most certainly a sight.

"The bathroom is just down the hall, second door to the left. Take the lamp, there's no window in there for light. Everything else should meet your satisfaction." *Indoor plumbing, thank the Lord*, she mentally praised. Agent Moore said she would have to adjust to using an outhouse. Thankfully, the agent had been wrong about that. "Up here, there is no gas lighting. Lamps must be used." She nodded.

"Thank you again for letting us stay here. I hope it won't be long."

"Not a problem." His rich voice softened.

"I think it would be best to establish which rooms are strictly off-limits, while we're here. I don't want to disturb your space." She shrugged, nervous being alone with a man she didn't know. "More than us being here already has, I mean." His forehead lifted mindfully, taking a good bit of dark hair with it. She hated the sound of her trembling voice.

"It is your home now too. Nothing needs to be off-limits, even to children." M.J.'s laughter rose up again. "It's good laughter fills these rooms again, even for a time." Her mouth opened, but nothing came out. "You should eat and rest a little longer before Edith Schwartz arrives." He made a motion to leave.

"Edith Schwartz?" She stared at the full plate on the bedside stand. Even the glass of milk looked tempting and she wasn't a fan of dairy.

"Joshua's wife. The bishop you met last night."

"Married us," she finished in a tone that even shocked her. It wasn't Daniel's fault she was here praising indoor plumbing and asking about boundaries instead of back home with a fully intact family, but someone needed to know she wasn't happy about this witness-protection arrangement and now that she was rested and fully alert, Daniel was the only one standing here. In her right mind, she would have never agreed to marry a stranger. It had all happened so fast, and in her delicate shocked state, she had numbly followed whatever Bryan felt was best for her children. Now, it all seemed too ridiculous for words.

"I'm sorry, I know that must have been difficult for you, but the marshal felt it was the best place to keep you all hidden. Our faith doesn't allow for a man and woman to live under one roof, unwed. But your children will be safe, fed—" he glanced at her food tray "—and given a place to heal, for however long you need." He didn't address her snarky tone, which surprised her. Whatever she thought, felt, he was being kind.

"I'm sorry too." And Magnolia was. This fake marriage wasn't only something she had to accept. He did too. Marriage was a sacred thing. She thought of Micah, how he'd wanted to leave and break that union. She had begged him not to let their children be raised in a broken home. He had acquiesced to her, but nothing was the same afterward. He lived his own life, she lived for her children, and for six years, passing a kind word had become her normal. Some men had so much, and yet wanted something different and Magnolia just wasn't new or different enough.

She considered the man before her again, this time for something more than his chosen apparel and the way he fit into it. This stranger was helping her without any reward, any reasoning. No one did something for nothing. Her eyes suddenly widened at the thought. Did he think he would be gaining a true wife with this arrangement? "What does this faith of yours expect from me?" Magnolia asked.

He again lifted that strong dark brow, measuring her meaning. It was a good look on him, if only aimed at another. "The truth?"

"The unedited version would be appreciated," she said in a professional tone.

"We have a set a rules, our *Ordnung*, which we each strive to follow. Our faith is the very center of our lives. The way we dress, how we do things, and even how we deal with others, are important." He shoved both hands into his pockets and lowered his gaze. "Edith will help with much of this. What being separate from the world truly means." He let out a sigh and looked to her again. "Mrs. Reynolds, I don't expect anything from you, if that is what you mean. You are only my wife, my *fraa* as we say it, in public. Here, you may speak plainly, live without expectations. We will work together to take care of your children, help them fit in here. Keep them safe until this man is caught."

She held his gaze a bit longer. He made it sound simple. This was all far from simple. Hannah wanted to believe him to be a man of his word, but then again, she was the worst judge of character on the planet. Micah had proven trustworthy, romantic, until Catherine came along, then he'd made work his priority. By the time M.J. was born, he put his work and his secrets first. And no matter how much she gave to him, the further he slipped away from her. She had kept her vows, remained the dutiful wife. And now, he was gone. She wasn't sure what she was supposed to feel about that aside from guilt. *If she had only been a better wife. If he had only been a better man.* The thoughts battled in her head.

"Thank you." She lowered her head, not wanting to linger on the subject long.

"Edith will be here shortly, as I mentioned. She will help you and the children…navigate. You will need to dress Amish first." He turned away but she didn't miss the spark of amusement before he did. "I am a fair hand in the kitchen and can handle a few meals, but I own a lumber mill." He turned to the window and pointed. "Just over that hill. I have two men who work with me. When you are more settled, I will introduce you. It would be good to have plenty of eyes looking out for each of you." Hannah didn't want any more eyes on them. The fear that even here, in the middle of nowhere, the wrong set of eyes might find them sent a chill up her spine.

"Our nearest neighbors are less than a mile

that way." He pointed in the other direction. "The Troyers. They have a large orchard, and Millie is a very kind woman, a widow with daughters herself. If you are here long…" He paused, clearly hoping that wasn't the case. "If you're here long, Millie would be a good friend to talk to, but only the bishop and Edith can know the true reasons for your being here."

"Of course," she hastily said. "We won't be talking to anyone if we can help it. I don't need any friends, just my girls kept safe until all of this is over."

"Again, I'm sorry for your loss. I will do what I can to make it more bearable being here," Daniel said. He headed for the door again.

"Oh, and I can cook," she quickly shot out. "Isn't that part of an Amish wife's duties? I'm not sure what Amish eat but…"

"The kitchen is yours then," he said, slightly amused. "I need to run to the mill and get a few things in order, but we will have the rest of the weekend to get each of you settled, find a routine. Routines are good, I think." He paused. "Don't let the *kinner*, the children," he added for her benefit, "go to the barn."

"Why? Is it dangerous?" She looked out the window for the barn. It was brick red and massive, near three stories high. In the storm last night, she hadn't a clue it even existed. Still, how had she missed such a structure?

He laughed, jerking her back to his attention. "*Nee*. I just have four pesky goats I really don't need M.J. falling in love with before I get them rehomed. I never saw a child so eager for my pancakes. I reckon animals might send her overboard." He chuckled again and strolled out the door. So Amish men had humor, could muster up pancakes, and didn't walk around frowning and carrying pitchforks.

She grinned. Glancing out the window, she nibbled on a slice of bacon. The barn was even bigger than the house and Daniel was right. M.J., as her little Sadie was now called, didn't need to see any goats. If he owned a cat, she could only imagine what would happen. It was sweet M.J. had already gotten to the man in charge of their care. In fact, the way he'd addressed Rosemary last night had taken her by surprise. Of course, he knew most of their situation, but he also took the time to be patient, speak slowly and bend to her level so as not to frighten her. Almost as if he wanted her to know she was safe. If he had regrets for helping them, it didn't show. But the question still lingered there. How did the US Marshals find an Amish man willing to take them in? After pulling her hair into a ponytail and picking up the tray, Hannah went downstairs to join her daughters.

"Morning, girls." Hannah sat the tray down where three little girls ate busily. Despite the churning in her belly, she ran on automatic. Mothers didn't have the freedom to wear their emotions freely. She needed her children to feel safe and establish normalcy as quick as possible.

"Morning, Momma," M.J. greeted cheerily. The scent of fresh coffee permeated the kitchen. She glanced around, searching the many cabinets and drawers for a coffee mug. Daniel opened the next cabinet, reached in and revealed a dark brown cup. Hannah offered a sideways smile of gratitude.

Daniel wasn't sure what he'd expected when he promised to care for Michael's wife and children, but now that he had a few hours' sleep and a better handle on everything, the petite blonde who sold real-estate in Indiana looked far from what he would have predicted.

Hannah entering his kitchen last night, draped in children, he hadn't been overly shocked to find she was pretty even with all she was enduring. Michael had always been more taken with outward appearances. Her fragile state of vulnerability matched a look of one tragically consumed with exhaustion. Dark circles under blue, watery eyes revealed fatigue and fear, making him want to offer assurances he couldn't. He was but one man, human, and full of flaws and forced to recognize his own disheveled state. Now on a new dawn, she was beautiful. They had both somewhat rested and had a duty to do. He still wasn't sure how any of this was to work, but a glance toward her plate, he noted she had eaten most of the food he had prepared. It was a start.

Living alone for so long he wasn't used to having others about. It would take some getting used to, but he would take his time getting to know them individually and making them feel at home.

"It's not Starbucks, but it will do," Daniel muttered haphazardly as she took her first sip of his muddy morning brew.

"You know what a Starbucks is?" Hannah questioned too hastily, her eyes widened in surprise. He gave her a half-hearted grin. She would be shocked if she knew just how much he knew of the world. He could tell her, but talking about that time in his life stirred up too many painful memories.

"I don't like this. You always make our breakfast," Catherine interrupted, pushing food around her plate as if it might be poisonous.

Daniel gave the eldest another long look. She had inherited her mother's coloring, but that cold stare she was gifting him was familiar, taking him back in time.

From what he learned last night, Catherine was nine. Coincidentally, the same age he was when his life changed too. He mentally stashed away that bit of information, hoping as the days passed he could use that to reach common ground between them.

At nine, his father had lost his faith and found living Amish too constricting, too suffocating. Dan Raber packed up his family, abandoned his faith, and moved them to a world that was flashy, fast, and tempting. In the end, that world had swallowed up everything Daniel loved. He seldom gave in to thoughts of yesterday, but seeing Catherine exhibit the same angry emotions he once felt, only reminded him that much more of the family lost to him too.

"I'm sorry about that, baby. It won't happen again." Hannah sat the cup down and went to her daughter. "I just overslept, but don't worry, I will be making all your meals from now on." Watching Hannah try smoothing out Catherine's rebellion, Daniel thought of his *mudder*. She never wanted to leave her upbringing, her family or the steady faith she had clung to until the end. Mothers were strong like that. At least Catherine had had Michael. He had obviously turned his life around becoming a man upholding the law, nothing like their own father. Forgiveness was essential, but part of him knew he may never be able to forgive his *daed* for taking them away from their Amish home. But he was here now, and so was Michael's family. Here, faith, family and community were the backbone of life. Here brothers didn't run away and stores weren't robbed. Lives weren't taken for a mere 209 dollars. Here, little girls didn't lose fathers to men like Corsetti.

"He doesn't even know what we like. We could have been allergic to something." Catherine slammed down her fork jerking Daniel back to the present. "What if he killed us?" Daniel remained unaffected in the outburst, though when Rosemary burst into tears, he wanted to go to her.

"That's being a bit dramatic, is it not?" Hannah said in a more firmer tone as she scooped Rosemary into her arms. "Mr. Raber worked hard to provide this meal for you and you will say thank you," Hannah ordered. Catherine mumbled a thank-you before sliding her plate away.

"Mommy, Mr. Raber said I can help milk a cow if you say it's okay," M.J. said with a mouth full of pancake, syrup dripping off her fork in a thick stream.

"Don't talk with your mouth full, Sadie."

"It's M.J. 'member?" her daughter scolded. "We got to learn our new names, Mommy. My new name is pretty, and I like it." Daniel stifled a laugh. The child had some charms, turning grown men into mush with smiles and an "I like it" stamp of approval for new things. Daniel knew from the moment they shook hands, he was done for. How was it even possible for a man to feel such love for children he just met?

And how fitting M.J. had been given the very name of her own grandmother. Martha was a common Amish name but what were the chances she had been given this one? Someday Daniel hoped to tell them each about the woman who'd left her mark on them, because it was as plain as the nose on his face; *Mudder* marked them all.

"Of course it is, pumpkin. I will try harder to remember your new names." Hannah eased Rosemary back into her seat now that she had calmed, and turned back to him. Daniel quickly withdrew his current infatuation with her five-year-old when she bore a perplexed look his way. "And I thought they weren't to go to the barn."

He offered her her forgotten cup of *kaffi*.

"I don't mind showing her the barn and an old milk cow before heading to the mill. This evening, I think it best to show you all around the property." He sipped at his cup, looking over the rim at her children. Rosemary glanced up, catching his attention. She was the spitting image of the grandmother she would never meet. The knowledge pricked his heart. Her fingers toyed nervously with the dark braid hanging over her shoulder. He'd give her a wider berth. Allow her all the time she needed to get settled. The marshal had told him she'd seen Michael's murder and had since not spoken a word. He knew so little about how such traumas affected the young, so little about children in general, but he knew time and prayer had ways of healing most of what plagued a soul and he would be sure to give her both.

"That's not necessary. Thank you for the offer but the children and I can stay right here until..." The sound of buggy wheels on gravel outside brought Hannah to alert. In her sudden jolt, she nearly dropped her coffee cup.

"It's just Edith Schwartz." Daniel reached out, touched her elbow with his palm to steady her. Her panicked look sent an unreasonable chill over his bones. "The bishop's wife. Remember?"

"I'm sorry, it's just..." Her voice trembled

and she glanced over to her children. Daniel couldn't ignore the matching looks spreading on their small faces.

"You are safe here. All of you." He looked toward the table to include each of them. *Assurances. They needed assurances.* "No harm will come to you here," he said without an edge of doubt.

"But, Daniel," Hannah whispered as Catherine resumed complaining over her eggs and M.J. boasted about getting to milk a cow beside them. It seemed those two had complete faith in his words, but Hannah was not so convinced. "I don't mean to offend, not when you have been kind enough to take us in, but you're Amish. If danger does come, how can I…"

"Defend your family alone?" he quickly put in. "You'll never have to know." Had she already forgotten his promise to her, the oath they swore by? "Hannah." Her name came on a promise that he hoped she understood. She wasn't alone to face what threatened. "No one is coming through that door that I don't invite in." With that stern promise, Daniel sat his cup aside and brushed past to let the bishop's wife in. He hadn't expected to feel this protective need or how Hannah's eyes pleading up to him would make him feel. Daniel exhaled a breath and reached for the door handle. He hoped if the need ever did present itself, he could make good on his promise.

Chapter Three

Edith Schwartz walked in the door, and was ready to get to work. Dressed in a rich blue dress and white apron front, she quickly lifted her black bonnet revealing a white smaller one underneath. Hannah wasn't sure what the purpose of two head coverings were. In less time than it took to pour a second cup of coffee, the healthy-framed woman walked into the kitchen, sized up Hannah and her daughters, and said, "Now let's get to making you each look more... Plain." With a toothy smile, she urged them all up the stairs. Edith knew all about their circumstances, Daniel had said, and she had offered quick condolences, but she wasn't the type to dwell, and quickly introduced them all to the Plain life.

Hannah heard the door downstairs shut. Daniel had finally left to see about his mill nearby. She appreciated all he was doing but having him breathing over them would become a nuisance. She'd had plenty of that with the US Marshals.

In the shared bedroom, full light exposing the layers of dust on the windowsills and bedside stand, they gathered. M.J. was already trying to sneak a peek into one of the bags Edith carried with her and distributed on the bed. "Patience, *liebling*." Edith patted M.J.'s curly head, affection glinting in her soft brown eyes.

"Many will be disappointed to know you have married our Daniel," Edith said as she emptied the first bag. She held up a length of material the color of the sky right before dark clouds rolled in, a rich blue hue. "A man with so much to offer is much sought after among the unwed *maedels* of our community," Edith said with a pleasant candor. Hannah couldn't help but feel Edith didn't approve of one of their own marrying an outsider.

"He has been very kind to help us," Hannah replied, though she wondered what Edith's thoughts truly were considering her marriage of convenience. Accepting the dress, she kept the question to herself and slipped into the neighboring room to change. She listened to Edith speak to her children in a grandmotherly tone through the walls. Just like her, her children had never known their grandparents. Edith's accent was much richer than the man she had married.

Hannah slipped out of her two-day-old jeans and shirt, neatly folding them as if just pulled from the dryer. Slipping into the dress Edith had brought, Hannah realized there were no buttons to secure the upper half of the dress closed. She gathered her dirty clothes into one arm and held her dress front with the other, then looked up and went rigid. It seemed the neighboring room was by all accounts Daniel's room.

Unlike the room she and the children shared last night, this one was smaller. Masculine, yet simplified. A tall dark stained wooden dresser and shorter matching one sat along one wall, beautiful doilies, handmade and slightly yellowed with age, draped over their tops. The large bed was made up, striking her as fascinating, considering Edith had only just arrived and Daniel lived alone. Micah had never made a bed once in their ten years of marriage.

The bed was draped in the most beautiful quilt she had seen in years. Blues and whites and a few shades of green arranged into a simple block pattern with a dizzy blend of mint and baby blue trim. Even a few feet away, Hannah could see the hand stitching. Mrs. Clayborn, the only foster mother Hannah had ever considered to resemble a mother, had loved to quilt and even taught Hannah a thing or two about tight stitches and proper binding. She didn't dare step closer, though she was eager for a closer look. On tiptoe, she stretched her neck to better view everything. On the bedside stand, there was a small black clock, wind-up style with bells on top. A small dish of change to the right and a long flashlight lay between the two. A man's room indeed, she thought, studying the naked windows in full morning light, breathing in the heavy scents of man and wood. It was a foreign mix, but surprisingly memorable.

The sound of M.J. in the next room, going on and on about her anxious need to have her first barn adventure, jerked Hannah's attention back. She hurried back into the room. Edith was helping M.J. into a soft blue dress slightly tattered at the hemline, while Catherine stood nearby, wearing a darker blue shade, arms crossed in an obvious temper. Her eldest had never known the feel of second-hand clothes before and it showed.

"And Mr. Raber says we don't give cows names because we eat them." Hannah wondered if Daniel perhaps had another dresser, somewhere, and then noted she needed to see her girls had a few extras, underwear, toothbrushes and so forth, as well. She had barely had time to pack what they needed. If they were going to spend the next few weeks here, there were essentials needed. Bates had given her plenty of cash with conditions she would let him know when she needed more.

"This is true. Now look at you. You look like a real Amish *kind*," Edith praised. "That means child." Edith winked. Hannah looked over the final results of her children's new identities. Who would have thought they could get more beautiful than they already were? She nodded her approval to each set of eyes looking to her for praise.

"Well, don't you look nice too," Edith said to Hannah.

"I didn't see any buttons." Hannah shrugged, revealing she was literally holding her dress together.

"Buttons aren't permitted here. They are considered showy and brazen. *Hochmut*. We are permitted to use hooks and eyes on dress backs and such, but I brought pins for that, dear." Hannah's eyes went wide. *Pins*. "Don't look so worried. Amish women have been wearing pins for centuries." Edith smiled amusingly. "This dress belonged to a new *mud-*

der with a *boppli* herself. It is a practical fashion for such, but I will see you have one like mine soon. I already cut out the pattern, along with a simple chore dress."

Edith helped Hannah pin her front so she wouldn't draw blood every time she moved. The children's dresses were simply pullover fashion. For that, Hannah was thankful.

"But, Ms. Edith." M.J. tugged at Edith's apron front. "If she is a milk cow, we won't eat her, will we?" M.J. was not one to let a thing go until it was fully understood.

"*Nee*, we need their milk." M.J.'s smile returned with that fact. "You must convince Daniel to let you meet her and name her properly," Edith said, tapping her nose. "Now sit on the bed and let's see about taming those sunshine curls of yours."

"I was going to name her anyway." M.J. bounced onto the bed, happy for all the extra attention Edith was showing her. "You think my hair looks like sunshine?" Hannah and Edith passed smiles. Martha Jane was beyond her years and stubborn to a point, but like most females, loved being fussed over.

"This looks stupid." Catherine stomped out, the door of the bathroom down the hall slamming shut soon after. Hannah walked over and picked up the prayer covering she'd tossed in her rant. This caused Rosemary to start crying. Torn, Hannah pulled Rosemary into an embrace. Catherine always took her time dealing with change.

"It's okay, baby. How about you sit on the other side of the bed, and Mommy will fix your hair." Rosemary nodded, and Hannah thumbed away her little tears. Rosemary's long locks, the color of Micah's, felt like satin against her fingers. She worked it into a braid, listened for Catherine down the hall with one ear and Edith's instructions with the other. Hannah formed a dainty braided bun held by three bobby pins before finally speaking.

"I'm sorry. It has been a lot to take in for her," Hannah apologized for her eldest daughter. Catherine had a mind of her own and it took an act of nature to bend it from its own thinking. Time was her only friend now, Hannah knew. And just as Rosemary had been affected by witnessing her father's death, Catherine had been the one to keep M.J. hidden upstairs and safe until help arrived. For that, Hannah was thankful Catherine had kept her head and protected her sister. Each child was different, had their own way about them. It was best not to push her eldest, but simply remain present until she came to you. Still, Hannah ached to hold her, bring her to her chest and show her all would be well soon enough.

"She is hurting. It is to be expected. Little girls are not meant to shoulder such things. There is much healing needed here." Edith glanced around the room. "You will all find that soon enough," Edith said with a firm certainty that had Hannah almost believing her. "We can wait for wearing the *kapps*. I should have considered how different this would be for you and brought kerchiefs instead. *Jah*, that would be best. Except when going out, you see." She pointed a finger. "Then the prayer *kapp* is necessary." M.J. hopped down and so did Rosemary. "Now your turn." Edith held out an arm in invitation and Hannah sat down obediently. No one had ever done her hair before, at least not since she was thirteen.

"Can we play in that empty room?" M.J. pointed and Hannah nodded her approval. The room was dusty, but bare, and close enough Hannah could hear them.

"Explain the dress, the head covering to me, the reasoning of it. I know being set apart is important."

"An Amish woman dresses plain to promote modesty. It is the same with covering our heads. To stand apart from the rest of the world, and yet not attract attention." Edith grinned at the irony of her own words. "A prayer *kapp* is not only meant to cover our uncut hair. We are to not wear our hair down, except with our husbands." Hannah sucked in a breath. No way would Daniel be seeing her hair down for however long she was to be here.

"It is also to remind us."

"Remind us?"

"To pray, always. To pray about everything and to step in Christ. Everything we do, our discipline, rules of our *Ordnung*, is to strive to live as simple and pure a Christian life as we can. To submit to His will. Now we make mistakes, like all, and must repent for them, but we are not so different. Tell me, Hannah, are you a woman of faith?"

"I must admit it has been hard. Micah, my husband, never encouraged it, but I was baptized when I was younger and took the girls each Sunday to a small church a few blocks from our home. I know much of the Bible but not well enough to recite verses on demand," Hannah said.

"Your husband did not attend church services with you?" Edith asked while reaching for the brush beside her.

Hannah laughed. "No. Micah was not interested."

Edith began working out the knots and kinks

of three-day-old untended hair. "The Lord kept you close to Him, and now you are here, with us."

"He had nothing to do with that," Hannah said to her. God didn't take fathers from children. Killers did.

"Oh, but He brought you here for a reason, *jah*? You could have gone anywhere. It is a big world and yet you are here. *Gott* always has a plan." Edith smiled coolly and slipped the stiff *kapp* over Hannah's head. "Now you look as you should. The heart will simply follow," Edith remarked, gathering up bags off the bed. Hannah wasn't quite sure what she meant but didn't want to offend by asking. There was much to learn about these people, their ways. Edith was being so kind and helpful. Hannah was grateful God had heard her prayer, bringing her and the children someplace that felt safe and kind.

"Let us start this day with a list of things you will need, and then tidy the *haus*. Daniel is not much for dusting, I see." Edith laughed, heading downstairs.

"I'm not sure a fake marriage and false names is what God wants," Hannah said, following faithfully behind. "But I do trust that the Lord knows best," Hannah told Edith as she followed her down the stairs.

Edith slipped into the kitchen, bustling about, putting things in order. "*Gott* always knows best. You will see." She smiled cunningly.

Hannah stiffened. "Daniel seems like a nice man, and I hope this doesn't tarnish his reputation or chance to find the real thing. I do have every intention of having our marriage annulled as soon as I can." Hannah hoped Edith believed her.

Edith pulled open a drawer and retrieved a pen and paper.

"What *Gott* brings together cannot be separated. If and when you leave, to Daniel, to the eyes of our community, and *Gott*, you will always be his *fraa*. Can you give me the *kinner*'s shoe sizes?" Hannah was in shock at her bombshell statement.

"No divorce?" Hannah buried her face into her palms as the reality of what Daniel had sacrificed hit her. She thought they would simply get an annulment and all of this would be a thing of the past once the authorities found the man who killed Micah, and her daughter was safe.

Edith reached across the table and took her hand. "Daniel is a *gut* man who will treat you all with respect and kindness. Your *dochdern* need a *daed*'s love and gentle hand." Edith patted her hand and smiled. "If this helps you, our Daniel has never courted anyone before." Edith chuckled. "I tried my hand at matchmaking, and failed. He agreed to this for your *kinner*'s sake, *jah*. He has offered his home, his name, to you and to them. That is something to respect and be thankful for." Hannah was thankful, but had no desire to stay here forever, as Edith was suggesting.

"He will provide for you and keep you safe for as long as necessary and you will learn how to care for his needs, as well. I will teach you this, *jah*?"

Daniel had promised them safety, but acknowledged they would eventually leave. He'd promised she was his wife only in public. Why hadn't he mentioned their marriage could not be annulled? "Edith, what kind of man would give up his life for strangers?"

"The best kind," Edith replied with a tender smile and another pat on Hannah's hand. "But he didn't give it up, as you mean. Daniel simply added to what was already here. This house needs what you have brought."

Hannah still couldn't believe it. What kind of woman became a widow one day and three days later a bride? Shame washed over her, despite knowing it was all necessary.

She went to the stove and poured herself

a third cup of coffee. She offered Edith one, which she graciously refused. Hannah sat back down and took a sip of coffee. Her heart was broken for the man she had loved, her stomach was nauseous at the betrayal he had delivered. Now she was responsible for ruining another man's future. How did one handle such emotions without the need to scream?

Chapter Four

For the rest of the day, Edith instructed Hannah how to use the washer ran by a gas-powered motor that was so loud Edith's instructions came in shouts. Hannah learned how to ring out clothes and hang them on the clothesline Daniel had outside the back door between T-shaped posts. Who would have guessed clothes had to be hung a certain way; but according to Edith, they did.

Out here, she caught a glimpse of the small garden of flowers where marigolds brightened the crisp, late, foggy morning. A single rose bush stood out at the corner of the house, yellow canary blooms thick as ants on a picnic basket of sweets. Strange to see such beauty this time of year. Hannah couldn't remember the last time she stopped and simply smelled the roses.

They dusted and mopped, ate peanut butter and jelly sandwiches, and on occasion laughed at something Edith said. Each girl helped, eager to please the woman dressed plain and ordinary, but clearly Edith was extraordinary.

Daniel's house was large, two full stories of dark, dusty rooms and sparse furniture. Old bookshelves in the sitting room revealed a man who liked to read more than just scripture. She'd spotted three Bibles in her ventures so far, and one old book that she couldn't tell what language it was but held the same worn-out appeal. She noted *The Count of Monte Cristo* and *A River Runs Through It*. Hannah had read those, but only because a teacher suggested them once. Her reading preferences leaned more toward romantic fiction where every ending was a happy one.

The upper-level rooms consisted of five bedrooms. She didn't figure her children would leave her shared bed for months, possibly years, and that was fine by her. There was one full bath and hallways that carried sounds far too easily. She liked the simplicity of it all. Primitive, yet functional. She didn't mind having no ties to the outside world. Not only was it safer, but it was quieter. It felt strange not to have her cell phone, but she understood why the authorities had insisted she toss it away.

, inhaled a deep breath and slowly let it
The world had never been so peaceful, so
"Thank you, Lord," she whispered.
Mom!" Catherine shouted from the other
of the screen door. Hannah jerked back
attention and hurried inside. "Where's the
? I looked everywhere and can't find it."
fore Hannah could answer her nine-year-
, Rosemary started crying. She did that at
st twice a day. Raised voices, tight spaces,
all seemed to be the new normal Hannah
ould have to help her adjust to. Hannah hur-
d into the kitchen, sat down her coffee and
ickly scooped the six-year-old into her arms.
atherine fussing, Rosemary crying, and M.J.
atching it all with big sad brown eyes, Han-
h simply reminded herself to breathe. This
as their new normal. They would adapt, just
she would. At least, this time Hannah hoped
e could.

"It's okay, baby. I've got you. We're safe,
oslyn. No one is here and we are safe. Just
reathe." It took little effort to calm her in her
rms, and within a minute, Rosemary was rest-
g against her mother's chest as they rocked
ack and forth in the chair at the kitchen table.

"Mommy, goats! Aren't they pretty?" Han-
ah turned to the kitchen door leading out of
e side of the house where her five-year-old

The house was also empty of life. Well, she
could add a large heaping spoonful while she
was here, as Edith mentioned. Throughout the
next hour, she forged on, wiped away years
of dust and neglect, and emptiness. No matter how she felt, Daniel had indeed sacrificed
for them and put his own future in peril. She
would do her best, with what time she had, to
show her appreciation.

She filled a fresh bucket of water at the sink
and thought about him, the stranger she was
chained to for the foreseeable future. Daniel's
eyes had glinted slightly when he mentioned
laughter was missed here. Hannah wondered
how much laughter once filled it. He knew so
much about her, but she knew nothing about
him. Edith said he never married, nor held an
eye for another. *Not a widower.* She moved
to the stairway, her small bucket of warm
water and wood oil soap mixture at her side,
and began washing the railing and delicately
curved spindles.

He wasn't that old, no wrinkles or touches of
silver. Daniel was rather nice-looking too. She
moved down to the next step, dipped her rag
in the bucket and repeated the same motions.
Daniel was a business owner, had a mill somewhere over the hill where four horses grazed.
So why, she asked herself, didn't he have a

wife and children to fill his big empty house? Wasn't that one of the most important things to the Amish aside from God? Family?

She shook her head. It was none of her business, she reminded herself. Daniel had indeed sacrificed his own future to protect her and her children. She would never wrap her head around that one, but she would repay him best she could. She would learn to clean and polish and cook like an Amish *fraa*, put on the proper appearances when in certain company and hope their suffering would end soon.

By evening, Hannah had a meal cooking in the oven and a kettle of coffee percolating on the back burner. This was as close as she could get to normal, for the sake of her children who needed normal badly. She had watched Edith climb into a small buggy and leave, promising to return again tomorrow and the next day, until Hannah was at ease with her new life. She had silently thanked God that He had sent someone to show her the ropes. She had a list of supplies on the table, a few recipes Edith knew by heart and three little girls who now had a glimpse of what having a grandparent felt like. To see actual smiles on their faces was enough to push her forward, accept this deception of pretending to be an Amish family.

She looked down at her feet. The bulky plain

black shoes Edith brought sur[...] fectly. They beat three-inch h[...] the week. She wasn't going to [...] tor job or the apparel it demand[...] made her smile. Then again, H[...] did appreciate the little things.

With the girls content playing [...] of cards found tucked in a drawer [...] ies, screwdrivers and other handy [...] nah stepped out onto the long front [...] swing in the far corner seemed a n[...] enjoy a fresh cup of coffee.

Fresh sheets blew on the line, t[...] scent carrying around the house, i[...] Two large oaks stood gallantly in th[...] shuddered in the late-September [...] glanced down at one hand, the dried [...] cleaning and washing all day. No st[...] hard work, there was something sati[...] it that she couldn't explain.

Seeing no threats immediately lur[...] allowed herself to relax a bit more ag[...] swing. A rooster crowed, though it wa[...] sunrise nor sunset, startling her. She [...] she would be a bit jumpy for days to c[...] chuckled at herself. No one would dare[...] them hiding so far off the beaten path[...]

The late September air was cooler t[...] last few days had been, and she clo[...]

was currently hugging a strawberry red goat munching on what looked like yellow roses.

Rosemary suddenly perked up at the sight of their newest visitors. "Come on, girls," Hannah instructed on a frustrated breath. "Let's get this creature back to the barn before it decides to eat all the laundry I just washed."

Daniel veered down the long driveway with the newly purchased rope. All children like to swing, he thought, though he had few memories of such things himself. He looked forward to seeing the girls smile, and tasting whatever Hannah had cooked up in the kitchen.

Nearing the barn, Daniel pulled back on the reins, bringing Colt, his best buggy horse, to a halt. His brother's wife in a dark blue dress, a size too big from the looks of it, stood near the corner of the house, both hands planted firmly on her hips. To his right, Catherine, in matching Amish dress, ran around the back of the house and soon appeared out the other side chasing a goat, the nanny's Nubian ears flapping like a basset hound giving chase.

Daniel growled. How had those critters gotten out of his newest pen? On the porch steps sat M.J., smiling as wide as the Kentucky sky while his brown-and-white-spotted nanny munched on his yellow roses. If Daniel weren't mistaken, M.J. was feeding the blooms to the pestering critter, not confiscating them. The old bush had been planted by his *mudder* when he was just a boy. He quickly jumped out of the buggy, tethered Colt to the fencing and went to put an end to all the ruckus. It was time to seriously try harder ridding himself of those goats. They were getting overly fat on grain and great at masterful escapes. They ate too much, cried too often and the rose bush was the last straw. *Jah*, they had to go.

Laughter filled the air, crossing the yard and reaching the barnyard. Daniel's gait slowed as the sound scraped over him. Hannah's laugh was not something he'd expected from a grieving widow on the run, and he didn't know what to make of it. No matter his scrutiny of his brother's wife, the soft pleasant sound brought him a sense of nostalgia and something else— something unfamiliar.

Hannah stopped running, blew a strand of hair from her face and let out an exasperated breath. To his surprise, Catherine was laughing too, chasing the black nanny goat who Daniel considered the ringleader of the unruly lot. Hannah watched her daughter, a soft loving look on her face. It registered within him, and brushed against his heart. *Mudder* used to do that when watching him and Michael run about. A mother's love was an undeniable sight. The woman had gone to great sacrifices for her children. He watched a breath longer, undecided what to make of her. One thing he did know, her beauty couldn't be easily ignored. Daniel was a man open to beauty. A sunrise over the hill often made him take a few extras moments to thank *Gott* for His careful hand. When new life was born, as it was on a farm, it warmed him in a way few things in life could. Finally sensing his presence, she turned to him, shaking her head before running toward him. Daniel quickly collected himself. He had no right to be noticing such things about her. This was Michael's wife.

"*Pest* was too kind a word," she said breathless. "They ate two sheets. Ate them." Her voice pitched. "And that rose bush behind the house is done for. Rosemary is watching over two we managed to get into the barn. M.J. thinks that one is her newest pet. But that one—" Hannah pointed an angry finger toward the black nanny "—needs a lesson in manners. She might not have horns, but can butt just fine without them." Hannah absentmindedly rubbed at her hip as she looked over her shoulder to see that the old nanny wasn't rearing up for another attack.

Daniel suppressed a laugh. No, she looked

nothing like an *Englisch* businesswoman born in the city. In her pretty blue dress and apron, her crooked *kapp*, she looked like an angry Amish woman ready to strangle a goat. Helping them fit in wasn't going to be such a difficult task after all, which surprised him, and little in this world surprised Daniel anymore.

"I'll go get some feed. Usually works well enough." He stepped away before she could see he was smiling.

"I'll have supper on the table in a minute. Please send Roslyn—I mean Rosemary—inside," Hannah said on a hurried breath. He nodded and headed for the barn, a play of humor teasing his lips into a grin.

"Oh, and, Daniel," Hannah called out and he turned back to her. "Thanks for not laughing, out loud." She walked away, her two daughters faithfully following. He tried not to think about the way her hair had escaped her *kapp*, or the way she stubbornly marched when in a tiff. He didn't need to notice how easily she moved about as if she hadn't a care in the world. He needed to ignore how appealing such things were. Michael's wife, like his children, was his to protect, and that was that.

Daniel announced himself before entering the barn so as not to frighten Rosemary. She was the easiest to startle and required a patient hand. He hadn't expected to find her nuzzling Colt. She jumped back as if caught doing something unlawful. Daniel moved casually toward her, offered a genuine smile.

"His name is Colt. And he likes when you pat his nose like this." Daniel demonstrated, taking Colt's bridle. Rosemary reached up and did the same as he worked to unhitch him properly. "I'll pick up some carrots and you can feed him. He is very fond of carrots." She hesitated for a moment and then suddenly ran out of the barn and into the house. It seemed Rosemary held a fondness for animals, and no fear of them. Another thing he hadn't expected.

"One day at a time, Lord. One day at a time," Daniel whispered. Things didn't seem so grim now. God had made him strong, compassionate. He knew the pain of heartache. Michael's daughters needed him and if Daniel were being honest, he needed them too.

When he stepped into the house, Daniel was instantly hit with the smell of crisp lemon floors and fresh air. The aroma of warm chicken took that over quickly. A man could get accustomed to coming home to such smells. So Hannah could cook, as she'd said she could, and clean too, apparently. He would make sure to thank Edith properly for her help. He felt almost ashamed at how dusty the house had become, but a working man had little time for such tasks, and living with a sawmill nearby only made what little effort he gave in vain. Dust was inevitable.

"Mr. Raber, Mommy made chicken and dumplings. I got to help. Edith says I'm neutral."

"Natural. She said you're a natural," Catherine corrected her sister.

"And look." M.J. twirled wistfully, ignoring her sister's words, one blond curl hanging out of the confines of two perfectly aligned braids. "I'm a real Amish girl."

"And pretty as a sunbeam, I might add." He tossed Rosemary a smile and almost believed she would shyly return it but Catherine had brushed by her with a stack of plates and a frown. Unlike the mother, whom she shared those fair looks with, Catherine was determined to resist his friendship, and anything else that didn't represent their old life. She just needed more breathing space, he considered. Michael had been like that, tempered when confined. Perhaps seeing more of the farm would help soften her.

"I hope you like dumplings. Edith made fresh bread and we found canned peaches in your pantry. So I made a simple cobbler.

I didn't have an Amish recipe," Hannah stuttered nervously as she carried a large pot to the table. "I'm sorry. I hope mine is suitable for your taste." She didn't seem as guarded as she had when he'd left for work. Daniel couldn't ignore how often she used the words *I'm sorry* either.

As he went to the sink to wash up, Daniel replied, "Food is food, and it all looks and smells delicious. *Danki*, Hannah." When she ducked her head and began retrieving forks and spoons from his disorganized drawers, Daniel noted a hint of pride glint over her features. She was eager to please, even if he had a feeling she didn't want to. A natural born thing, he observed. Did she always blush when thanked or complimented? He aimed to find out. "The dress looks nice," he muttered beside her. "You will have no trouble fitting in to our community."

"Just part of the role," she shot back. A hint of warmth had pressed on her soft cheeks. *Jah*, he would have to thank Edith for much. Everyone seemed more relaxed, except for him. His brother's family was now, at least for now, his. Michael would be furious to know they were here, eating at the very table they once had, wearing the clothes he once wore himself.

Catherine reached for a slice of the fresh

bread. Daniel spoke up. "Catherine, we have prayer before we eat." The quicker they learned what was considered normal, expected, the faster they would take to it and avoid unnecessary attention.

"We did that at breakfast already," she shot back, not hiding her sharp tone.

"*Jah*, we did. There is no amount too great when it comes to prayer. The Lord has provided us with food to nourish our bodies. Some aren't so blessed. We have seen another day, and you are all here, safe and together. We have much to be thankful for."

"And Daisy. Don't forget we are thankful for Daisy," M.J. quickly added.

"Daisy?" Daniel queried, turning to Hannah.

"I had to take them into the barn to know where to put your pest." Hannah smiled knowingly.

"Milk cow," M.J. interrupted. "You said we can't name cows because we eat them. But Edith says we don't eat milk cows, which makes me happy. So I asked milk cow what she wanted me to name her and she said Daisy."

Hannah shot him a grin that said, *That's my M.J., try and tell her no.* Well, Daniel couldn't. Naming animals wasn't smart on a working farm, but what harm was it to name one if it made at least one child smile today.

"Well, if she said it was okay, then I can't go against it. I like Daisy. Now let's bow our heads and say a silent prayer." He leaned toward M.J. "That means we don't say our prayers out loud, but we should thank *Gott* for what we have been given." M.J. nodded hard, indicating she would follow instructions. Everything about the little one had his heart fluttering in his chest, filling empty voids that had long echoed with grief.

After the best meal Daniel had eaten in months, he stood from the table. "That was *appeditlich*, delicious, *danki*. After the girls help you clean up in here, I want to give them a tour of the farm."

"That isn't necessary," Hannah said and began stacking plates on top of one another. "We won't be here long enough to need a tour, and cleaning up is my duty, not the children's."

"We can't know how long you will be here. And children need something to do. It teaches them skills, and douses boredom," Daniel countered. Last thing he needed was four bored females wreaking further havoc on his life.

"I understand that is how things are done in your world, but not in ours," Hannah responded in a clipped tone. "And we don't know what's out there. It's best we stay inside, close to the house."

Daniel noted her rigid posture, her arrogant tone. Five seconds ago, she was smiling. He would never understand women. He didn't want to argue with her in front of the girls and he did understand her concerns, but it was important they each knew their surroundings. He had an old well and some of the fences were solar electric. Then there was the matter of the creek. Did any of them know how to swim?

"We live in the same world. Best to know your surroundings," he said before turning toward three sets of young eyes gawking at him. "Ladies, help your *mudder* clear the table and wash the dishes, then get on your shoes and meet me on the porch. We *will* be taking a little adventure." Now that he'd sparked interest in three little hearts, Daniel walked out the door. From what he could see so far, Hannah had a hard time saying no where her children were concerned. He wasn't the type to take advantage of a situation, but this time, he would. Outside, Daniel leaned against the railing and listened to the bustling indoors.

"Mommy, I want to see the farm and horseys and go on a 'venture." Daniel chuckled knowing he hit lit that spark and there was no way Hannah would refuse those big brown eyes.

"He called us ladies," M.J. went on, making Daniel smile.

"Dad would never make us do dishes," Catherine added. Daniel sighed heavily. It wasn't going to be easy, helping Catherine fit in, but he had made a promise to protect them, help them adjust and find healing, and he was a man who kept his promises.

Chapter Five

As the children finished drying dishes, Hannah stepped out onto the porch. Daniel was leaning against a porch post, taking in the horizon, its brilliant orange and red flames illuminating the sky. She took in a breath, never one who liked admitting she was wrong, and stepped forward. They had lived life a certain way—Micah's way—for so long, she hadn't considered it before now. Catherine didn't even know the basics of life, like washing dishes. What harm could be done seeing the farm? A walk would do them all good in truth.

"I understand about the girls needing things to do, but you must understand that my husband insisted that his daughters would never be treated like…"

"Like responsible and capable young women," Daniel tossed out quickly. He must have heard

Catherine's outburst. She met his slow lifted glare. "You are not the only ones having to adjust, Hannah, but if we are to make this look real, they have to do what other Amish children do. Chores would be good for them and will keep their minds off worrying."

"You're right," she said. "Busy is always best. It will simply take a bit of getting used to, perhaps."

"And hiding inside, never seeing sunlight, is no good for anyone." He was right again, and she hated it.

She didn't argue. "Things happened so fast, and when the marshals said this was our best option, I accepted that. I'm fine playing dress-up to fit a role, for their safety, but they didn't ask for any of this."

"I understand. Neither did you." His eyes held her captive for one shuddering minute before traveling down and pausing at the ring on her hand. The simple band, a forever promise melted into gold. Hannah stared at it with mixed emotions; anger, grief, a large dose of regret with a side helping of guilt. If she had been a better wife, maybe… She shook off the thought. Life had kicked her plenty enough to know control was never in her hands. *Adjust and adapt*, she reminded herself. And for now that meant keeping the peace and accepting new ways.

"I married a man who lied and stole and put us all in danger. I don't know that we need a tour of a farm we may not stay at for long. There's danger out there," she said, putting the ringed hand behind her back. She would need to remove her wedding band, for the sake of this lie, but it had been a part of her for so long. How did one just toss out the one thing meant to stay with you for a lifetime?

"So he was not a good man?" Daniel's jaw tightened. He was Amish, surely hearing about the things Micah had done troubled him. Hadn't Bryan given him all the facts surrounding the threat out there?

"It would seem he wasn't. That's why we should stay inside, away from dangers."

"The marshal gave me a number to call each afternoon to check in. They believe that man, Corsetti, is heading north." He paused, nodding to where north was. His dark hair held more curls than she'd noticed before, a ridged line where his straw hat sat. "I don't know how to convince you this is the last place anyone would look for you. You will have to trust me, Hannah. You are safe here."

She looked around, seeing only roads, fields and forest, and just one house in view.

"The *kinner* need to know where they are so they can explore, do little chores, feel part of something. They need to know about old wells to avoid, neighbors they can turn to. They need to be children." He looked to her again. How could she argue with someone who was right, about all of it? She wanted them to live in peace with a sense of normalcy too. She was smart enough to know she wouldn't find it, maybe ever again, but this might be as close as she would get for now delivering it to them.

"So do you have family up north?" He studied her with those fascinating hazel eyes. Probably to see her *kapp* was straight and her hair hadn't found its way out of the three bobby pins holding it in place. Could they really pull off presenting themselves as a family to others?

"A foster grandmother," Hannah replied. "She isn't really my family. I never truly knew her. The Thompsons never adopted me, really, just let me stay until I was of age to leave. The authorities already warned me they might head there first, but I haven't talked to her for over twelve years." She went to the railing, looked out at the long gravel drive, fencing aligning the sides. It was rural and earthy, serene.

"You were a foster child?" She detected a hint of surprise in his low tone. Micah always spoke louder than necessary, his words fast and hurried. Yes, everything here was slower. Maybe, after all of this was over, she could find a quiet little space in the world like this to raise the girls in. Some place small with few neighbors, but not fully detached.

"Three times over at least," she replied, leaning against the post opposite him and picking at her nail, removing more of the polish instead of looking at him, wondering what he must think. Then wondering why she cared what he thought at all. Surely, he knew nothing of the real world. The Amish had big families, and, as she was learning, big hearts. No way could Daniel understand her world when his was so quiet and peaceful, and safe.

"How did... Sorry. It's none of my business." He looked out again. Hannah studied his features, the slight hint of an afternoon shadow on his face.

"It's not one you could understand, given who you are," she replied awkwardly. Daniel turned to her again.

"You would be surprised, given who I am." He arched a brow, revealing a man who might be a bit of a mystery himself. "Do you think because I am Amish, I'm exempt from knowing how the world can be?" His arms crossed over his chest, signaling she hadn't a clue about his world.

"No… Yes. I don't know," Hannah scrambled. "I was told you lived among the English for a while, but not how long." But wasn't that something all teenagers did? What was it called…*rumspringa*? At least that's what Agent Moore had said.

"Long enough to know their ways, their reckless regard for others and that I didn't belong there." A thousand scenarios flashed through her mind. That's when she saw it, the pain those eyes carried between the flecks of gold. Right now, Daniel Raber didn't look like a stoic savior to her current woes but a man who had lived and loved and lost. There was more to this man than met the eye, that was for certain. One thing Hannah learned early on, was you didn't get something for nothing. If she wanted to know more about him, that meant she had to give something of herself up.

"I was given up by my mother when I was born and adopted by the Delaneys." His eyes remained on her, unflinching. "They couldn't have children, but when I turned four, Mrs. Delaney got pregnant after years of failed attempts. So I was no longer needed." She couldn't remember them, but she did remember the feeling of being pushed on to the next temporary home and the next. And all her years of trying to fit in, and be loved.

"Children are a gift from *Gott*. I will never understand some of this world."

"It's a waste of time trying. Anyway." She shook off the old memory. "I was passed around a bit, I don't remember how many times, but when I was seven Henry and Anna Clayborn became my foster parents." Hannah smiled, thinking of the couple who taught her how to bake cookies, catch fish and took her to church three times each week. "They were older, had lost their daughter, but I never felt like a replacement. Not to them." Their love for her was undeniable. "They were wonderful people." She toyed with her *kapp* strings as the breeze picked up, letting them tickle her neck.

"I'm glad you had them," Daniel said, studying her intensely. She never liked people who stared, making her uneasy, but with Daniel she didn't feel uneasy. Hannah felt…listened to.

"It was the happiest time of my life." Until she had become a mother. Nothing outmeasured the miracle of bringing life into the world.

"Are they still part of your life, your daughters' lives?"

"No. They are both gone now. Anna got sick when I was thirteen, with cancer." She glanced at her feet, ran her shoe over the planks nervously. "Social services removed me from their care and handed me over to the Thompsons. I never got to say goodbye to her. The one woman who loved me most in this world, and they didn't let me say goodbye." She didn't mean to cry, but losing Anna and Henry had been the hardest loss she ever endured.

"I'm sorry." Daniel offered her a handkerchief. Plain white, all but one little flower in the lower corner. Who even carried those anymore? Apparently, men like Daniel.

"Me too." She took a breath. "The Thompsons, home number three, were what we foster kids called kid collectors." Hannah shrugged. "They house as many children as the state allows, collecting larger checks, which is seldom spent on their wards. As soon as I came of age, I left and went back to find Henry."

"And?"

"He had passed too."

"You have lost much," Daniel said with sincerity but not surprise. She guessed right about that part. Daniel Raber understood loss well.

She hadn't a clue what possessed her to share so much with him. Perhaps it had been too long since she'd had someone who listened to her. Someone who wanted to hear her. It was sweet and, surprisingly, too easy. If she wasn't careful, Hannah might just start to consider Daniel a friend.

* * *

Daniel hadn't predicted Hannah had endured so much in her short life. He only hoped his brother had treated her better than those who'd come before him, but was realizing that might not be the case. No wonder her eyes lit up every time he offered a proper thank-you when she made a meal, washed clothes or swept his house. As far as her tidbits of information, he would speak to Marshal Bates about those. No one mentioned his brother had stolen from these men. The threat they were all hoping to avoid might be more dangerous than previously thought.

They both grew silent. The moment drifted into an unexpected intimacy, sharing emotional wounds, as each stood leaning on their own post with a few steps separating them. No more than four feet, but continents apart.

Daniel contemplated the best methods of closing the distance. The marshal insisted he withhold his connection to Michael for now. Hannah didn't need to know Michael had left his family at seventeen and never once called his grieving mother. When their parents died, Michael hadn't even attended their funerals.

She had shared something of herself with him in hopes he too would offer up something of himself in return. Daniel simply wasn't ready to open up as freely as Hannah had, but he pondered over the similarities they did share. He did know what it was like to move around, learn to adapt to new surroundings, and how it felt to not fit in.

After his parents' passing, Daniel had a few friends, a good job at Bentley's Construction, and he had tried to carve out a life for himself. But the city never stuck. He was always the odd man out, the orphan without roots. That's how he felt those years back, but it seemed Hannah had truly been the one without roots, the real orphan.

His mundane life took a pivotal turn the day he opened *mudder*'s Bible and found pages and pages of her heartfelt words, scribbled and tucked away. She'd described a life he had craved for, one he barely remembered, with rules and restrictions, and he wanted it. Without hesitation, Daniel traded the worldly for the simple. Here, in Miller's Creek, is where he belonged. So at twenty-five he packed up his scarce belongings, whispered a dozen prayers, and knocked on Joshua Schwartz's door. His *onkel* had just become bishop and not only remembered him, but welcomed him to the flock. Daniel gave up what he knew, gave in to what really mattered, and joined the Amish community of his roots. It was one brave act that led him here. Hannah had had to act brave most of her life, he was learning.

When the girls scurried out to them, he was glad for the distraction. Listening to Hannah talk about her upbringing made his childhood look like a flick of dust in her heavy dustpan. His father may have made life hard, his life uncertain, but his parents loved him and he knew they did. Daniel never felt unloved.

"Who is ready to meet David and Goliath?" Daniel announced. M.J. immediately threw up a hand, her big brown eyes full of wanderlust to see two big work horses. It couldn't be ignored how Rosemary timidly took in a breath and nearly smiled. He hadn't expected the bridge he hoped to build between them to be constructed so quickly. When it came to Catherine, he knew a lot more hammering would be in order. He just needed to find the right tools.

After a quick tour through the barn, introducing all the animals and explaining electric fencing, Daniel took them to the location of the old well. It was long dried up and forgotten but clearly a hazard to children. He would make arrangements to have it filled soon so as to avoid any accidents. Considering they were so close already, he turned northeast. Not toward home, exactly, but to the creek where willows and birch grew thick. He'd kept the path clear, mostly. There weren't many hours in the day to complete every duty. He walked ahead, smashing down any threats of briars or weeds that might slow their stroll and scratch small ankles. Cool air and the waft of water filled his lungs. How long had it been since he just took a walk? Whip-poor-wills called between frog songs and the first crickets of the season chirping.

"You have so many horses. Which is your favorite?" M.J. asked, stumbling along behind him, a shadow he found pleasing. He glanced over the parade, white *kapps* trailing one after the other as eyes marveled at the simplicities of the country.

"They are all important. David and Goliath are my stronger horses. They pull wagons and hay mowers and sometimes logs for my mill. Maybelle was my buggy horse for a long time, and now that she is getting older, I like to let her rest as much as possible. That's why I use Colt so often."

M.J. toddled up closer. Daniel slowed his gait near the tree line. "Rosemary likes Colt, but she won't tell you that. I like them all, even Daisy. *Mudder* says your barn is bigger than our house."

"Dirtier than it too, I imagine." Daniel shot

Hannah an apprecitve smile. She had in just one day restored the home of his childhood with scents that invoked pleasant memories.

"Can you milk a horse?" M.J. inquired.

Daniel whipped around abruptly. "*Nee.* We only milk cows." The things kids asked.

"Are there small cows you can milk? Like my size?" Daniel chuckled at her eagerness to try something new.

"*Nee.* I guess you can milk a goat, but that would mean they have to become moms first." Daniel regretted the remark as soon as it escaped his lips. M.J. lit up like a new spark on a dark night and opened her mouth but before she could spill out another question he wasn't prepared to answer, Catherine spoke up from behind them.

"What's that sound?"

"Don't tell me you don't know." Daniel grinned and slowly stepped out of the way. Like scared sheep, Hannah's daughters moved into the clearing. The moment their eyes discovered the source of the sounds, they went wide with excitement. The creek was gently flowing, trickling over rocks and pebbles in a cadence. A few cicadas welcomed them, droning their call. On the opposite side were deep enough depths for a summer swim, but Daniel kept to the shallow shore leading them to an open rock bed area. He should be mucking stalls, storing feed. Anything but this, but he had to admit that he too was enjoying a meandering walk through the woods and along the creek beds.

"Say." He turned to M.J. "Have you ever skipped a rock?" Anyone who didn't know what a creek was, he thought not. Days were warm but the nights were growing chillier. He wished he could strip them of their shoes, lift a few stones and catch crawdads, but he could see they were already spellbound. Simply pleased by this new wonder. Who would have thought such a simple stream of water could build more bridges?

Chapter Six

Just before 4:00 a.m., Daniel rolled out of bed. Sleep would not come easy, knowing so many were dependent on him. He stepped into his trousers, pulled on a fresh shirt, and quietly made his way down the hall.

He quietly brushed his teeth and splashed cold water on his face. *Kaffi*, he needed lots of caffeine today. Some of his *onkel*'s stout brew would come in handy right about now, he mused, scrubbing his hand down his face.

On the wide marble sink, he spied the razor and picked it up with one hand. But then he realized he was a married man now. Shaving wasn't necessary now that he was married. He stared into the small mirror, his reflection staring back at him. "What have you done, *bruder*?" he whispered. Michael had stolen. He'd put his children in danger. He'd left a wife, who had already seen her fair share of heartaches, with something else to shoulder. And now, his brother's sins were his to carry.

Daniel tucked the razor away in a dresser drawer, best to keep such things away from little fingers anyway, and made his way downstairs. He could have a day's worth of chores done before breakfast and it wouldn't hurt to take a look around, ensuring the safety of the farm. His life had been predictable these past few years, and now four females had changed that. Watching the children's faces light up, their curious natures flicker to life yesterday, Daniel felt a part of something he hadn't predicted. What it felt like to be a father. Their safety, as well as their happiness, meant a lot to him. It wasn't duty or obligation any longer. Was that wrong? He thought about that as he slipped quietly into his boots and out the back door.

Over the quiet weekend, Daniel had moved two dressers into the shared bedroom for Hannah to stow a few items in. She glanced down at her hand, turned the gold band counter clockwise twice, and slipped it off her finger. Jewelry, wedding bands included, wasn't permitted within the Amish. She tucked the ring under a few garments and shut the drawer. In a fast moving week, Edith had managed to gift them two dresses each, undergarments and shoes. Time flew by briskly in the shadow of chores and establishing new habits. Hannah liked routine. Routines promoted stability. As long as she was here, she might as well embrace it. *Until the next shake-up.* Because if there was one thing Hannah knew, life never let you get comfortable for long.

As she descended the stairs, Hannah thought about the meal she'd served tonight at dinner. Micah had had his preferences, what meals he wanted her to serve on a regular basis, but now, with Edith's generous contributions and a pantry filled with possibilites, Hannah was experimenting with new flavors. With so many fresh ingredients, peppers, onions, canned tomatoes, Hannah had added chicken, a healthy portion of spicy mustard she once read about in a magazine recipe and a light splash of vinegar. The stew was gold. If there was a food Daniel didn't like, Hannah hadn't found it yet. It took so little to earn appreciation here. Daniel always thanked her for every effort she made, even when she burnt toast without the convenience of a real toaster. She smiled, recalling a failed Sunday breakfast. Normally she would have been devastated to fail at something so small, but Daniel rushed into the room, flew

mile on his face as he looked over her
tle girls blissfully sleeping.

nk it's the highlight of their day actu-
de from going to the creek again," she
"I must say I have never skipped rocks

l, maybe we should do it again one eve-
Something in the way he suggested it
her off guard. Was skipping rocks reg-
part of his life?

u weren't very good at it, you know."
nned. Did he even know just how hand-
those grins were? "We could stroll over
chard fields next door. It's quite a sight
ng when it's in full bloom. They're har-
g now, which is wonderful to see too."
ey would like that," she responded. Dan-
ened his mouth to say something else,
osed it again. "So about the use of the
e." She moved toward the door and he
ved. "Can I do that soon?"

h, tomorrow around noon?" She hated
ay the dim lamplight made his eyes look
ntense.

oon?" she questioned.

ou can bring lunch for all of us. You
ld know Eli is allergic to peanut butter,
we Amish men will eat just about any-

open the windows, and instead of stirring up
a fuss, he laughed. Hannah was learning that
not all laughs were cruel. And oh, how she
missed laughter.

She slipped into the kitchen, poured a small
cup of coffee before rinsing out the kettle and
headed over to the sitting room where her girls
awaited Daniel's nightly reading of the Bible.
It too had become habit, his idea of normal.
Surprisingly, Hannah liked this routine just
as much as his nightly patrols of the farm he
hadn't a clue she was aware of. He sold her on
their safety here by remaining vigilant, con-
vincingly so, and Hannah watched out her window each night for his silhouette moving into
the barn, outbuildings and parcel before the
lock on the front door clicked to his satisfaction. It was comforting, his hedge of protection, and having an extra set of eyes watching
out for her children. She never thought trust
would come so easy with a stranger, especially
where her children were concerned, but Daniel
carried the very essence of trust, the perfect
partner to help her endure the coming days.

Hannah slid between Rosemary and Catherine on the long couch. She sat her cup down
as M.J. curled into her lap. The sitting room
was vast, open and airy with hints of mascu-

linity added. So much open space Catherine could do cartwheels, she mused.

Daniel read from the last verses of the Book of Ruth. Hannah remembered the story well. Ruth had suffered many hardships, but she had Naomi. Hannah had no one. Ruth had Boaz, though Hannah was skeptical. Boaz had looked out for Ruth, but hadn't he been rewarded with much land for marrying her? Hannah would never understand men, or love for that matter. Then again, she was no Ruth.

The slow timbre of Daniel's voice was easy to listen to. She had never known a man who read aloud other than the pastor at their small church. She caressed M.J.'s hair, let her mind recount the events leading her to this night, this place. From the moment the police appeared at her Realtor job to the rush into witness protection, a lot had conspired. In hindsight, Hannah was beginning to piece together why Micah had insisted on her returning to work and why he kept all their financial problems from her.

Daniel closed the Bible, jerking Hannah back to the present. "Let me help you carry them up to bed," he offered, setting the Bible aside and getting to his feet. She hadn't realized the time had raced by and now her daughters lay fast asleep.

"I know you speak to Marshal Bates, but

would you mind if I use
him myself?" Hannah g
positioned M.J. in her ar

Daniel gingerly lifte
the couch and offered he
shouldn't be a problem. I h
at the mill. I'm surprised y
to ask." So was she, but sh
with Edith, learning her w
had forgotten that she neede
Bryan herself, not just trust
her the most precise update
ing he kept things to himsel
had taught her many things,
their partners in the dark wa

"I don't like being a burden,
to talk to him. I've known Br
He and Micah were close frie

"You're not a burden, Hanna
anything." She wondered if h
that. Daniel seemed guarded w
himself.

They carried the children up,
a second trip to fetch Catherine
they tucked the girls under the
of the quilts she had found in a c
the other rooms.

"I think I bored them to sleep,

boyish
three l
    "I t
ally, a
added
befor
    "V
ning
caug
ular
    "
He
so
the
in
ve

ie
b
p
f

thing, as you well know." She fought the urge to shake her head at his cunning.

"Lunch?" Hannah crossed both arms but couldn't hide her amusement in his subtle request, or how much she really enjoyed his laid-back humor. If Hannah weren't mistaken, Daniel Raber was a bit of a charmer too. She would do well to keep things strictly friendly.

"You can use the phone and M.J. can entertain the men with stories about rock skipping and milk cows." Daniel moved through the doorway and turned back to her.

"I don't think that's a good idea, Daniel. The Marshals said the fewer people we meet the better."

"I think it's a fine idea. So bring us lunch tomorrow, use the phone and let me show off those pretty girls." He moved down the hall before she could even object. He said it as if he wanted to parade her children around, as his own. Part of her took offense. They were not his children, but Hannah couldn't help thinking, what would be the benefits of a father figure like Daniel for her girls? She shook the thought off quickly. None of this was real. Daniel was her husband in name only. A pretend father. She was leaving as soon as it was safe. He knew that. He agreed to it. No way could a man like that really want a woman like her. They weren't his, and neither was she.

Chapter Seven

"How's it feel being a married man?" Eli Plank elbowed Daniel as they finished stacking a lumber order for Lynch Construction.

"It's different," Daniel said honestly, ignoring Eli's wiggling brows. It was like being a fish out of water. What had possessed him to invite Hannah for long walks and lunches? Those soft smiles and two ovals of heavenly blue caused a man to succumb to a momentary weakness. He raked a hand through his hair. Eli poked him again and bellowed out a laugh. "I bet it is." Daniel handed both his employees a sports drink, and chugged his down like a man wandering the desert. He didn't want to talk about his complicated married life, wished he hadn't informed his hired hands about his newly acquired family, but he wasn't showing up for *Gmay*, the biweekly church service, with a family. Tongues would be wagging but Daniel knew, between Edith and Eli, the community would all know by now he was a married man.

Being responsible for Michael's family was a gift. At least that's what Joshua called it. Daniel didn't regret taking on the extra responsibility, but to them he was a stranger. A mere safe haven until the authorities took them away again. But Daniel was becoming attached. Each girl needed something different and he was edging closer to discovering what that was. He would never have children of his own, this being as close as he would ever get. When this was all over, he would tell them who he was, how they were connected. Hopefully, Hannah would allow him to see the children from time to time. They were becoming friends he liked to think. Surely, she wouldn't find a problem with that. Then again, it was Michael who had gotten her into this whole mess after all. Guilt took a stab at him. Would she sever their family ties once she discovered who he was?

"She a good cook? Nothing worse than marrying a woman and finding out she can't boil water." Eli's question interrupted him from his thoughts.

"That's poor Simon Beachy's problem," Vernon Schwartz added in. "He thought he was getting a jewel when he married my sister, Tracie. Found out soon enough she can't cook a lick. *Mudder* tried plenty. It never stuck." Vernon shook his light brown head in bewilderment. His straw hat shed a thick layer of sawdust into the breeze. Standing left of the mill usually earned him a good dusting of sawdust. "She can sew and grow just about anything, but can't fry an egg or bake a cake to save the farm."

"Well, Hannah cooks fine. Though she makes some dishes I have never heard of. She made pork with some barbeque sauce and ranch dressing mixture that was awfully *gut*. The woman liked her spices too." Daniel rubbed his belly. "I've no complaints in that department."

"And don't complain either. That doesn't work. Women don't have good ears like we do," Eli said. "Is she *schee*?" Hannah was more than pretty, Daniel wanted to say. "You *have* been keeping her hidden away for more than a week." Eli lifted a brow. "Makes one wonder."

"That isn't an issue," Daniel replied with a red-faced laugh. Hannah was beautiful, inside and out. "And is it not what's on the inside that counts?" Daniel poked back.

"That's what *they* say." Eli winked. "But it's

awfully nice if you can stand to look at her."
Vernon and Daniel laughed. They would both
see for themselves just what Daniel had gotten himself into in another hour or so. Edith
felt that slow introductions into the community were best, and with church Sunday in just
a couple days, Daniel hoped Edith was right.
Hannah was still tense, always looking over
her shoulder, waiting. Rosemary seemed more
relaxed outdoors, but every creak of a floor-
board drew her back. Strange, how indoors she
seemed skittish, while outside she let down
her guard.

"I will never understand why Sara ever
agreed to marry the likes of you," Daniel
teased. Sara Plank was too kind a woman to
be married to his bolstering foreman.

Eli gave Vernon a wink. "What about the
kinner? They growing on ya yet?" *Crawled
into his heart*, Daniel thought.

"They've been through a lot, losing a *daed*,
moving, getting a new one." But it was getting
better he believed wholeheartedly.

"Makes sense," Vernon said and went back
to stacking lumber.

"Hard thing, death. Especially on *kinner*.
They might need more time to adjust," Eli said
without any sarcasm.

"Not that little one," Daniel added. "I'm not

sure how to get through to the oldest two and Hannah is a bit protective. They have been a foursome for a spell. I don't understand all her ways of thinking." Like why the girls didn't need to do chores. Daniel suspected it had little to do with Michael and more to do with Hannah's need that her children not be subject to hard work. He tried seeing her side of it. Had her time as a foster child been all about work? Had she never been given a proper childhood of her own? He had his suspicions.

"Don't bother trying to understand women. Just be glad *Gott* created them," Eli advised.

Daniel chuckled. "You're probably right about that."

"Always am." Eli beamed arrogantly.

"I think your house full of women is about to get a welcoming they won't forget," Vernon added.

"Huh?" Daniel turned in the direction Vernon was nodding.

Eli burst into laughter. "Is it Tuesday already?"

It was clear to see lunch was now canceled thanks to his weekly visitor.

Hannah added freshly sliced cheese to each chicken sandwich currently spread out on the counter. She'd made chocolate chip cookies, baked beans, and managed to put together a small salad that included tomatoes, cucumbers and onions, with a homemade vinegar dressing. Her recent bread-baking attempt was a complete failure, but thankfully Edith had seen to it they had plenty to spare from their cooking practices. She would try again tomorrow, hating that she hadn't gotten the hang of something seemingly so simple with only four ingredients. Water, flour, yeast and salt, and she managed to ruin it.

Catherine tucked plates and forks into the large basket Daniel had laid out for her this morning as a reminder. The man wanted his lunch delivered. It was the least she could do, considering he was housing and providing for four extra mouths to feed.

"The mill will probably be dirty," Catherine quipped, always trying to find the downside to everything. Hannah ignored her. In fact, she looked forward to seeing where Daniel worked, how he spent his day. Just the walk over the hill alone would brighten her spirits. For as restless as her daughters were becoming staying near her side, under the cover of walls and doors, Hannah was feeling a bit restless too.

Daniel mentioned his hired hands during supper. Hannah learned that Vernon Schwartz was his fourth cousin and had four kids, all with names that started with *S*. The other man working under Daniel's employ, Eli Plank, was apparently full of bad advice, which he liked to give out for free and Daniel insisted no one should take. It would be a nice change of atmosphere, getting to know the people around her. She had lived in the same house for nearly seven years and hadn't even known the names of most of her neighbors.

At the sound of a buggy outside, Hannah's heart jumped into her throat. Her daughters too, came to alert. "It's just a buggy. Nothing to worry about," Hannah assured them as much as herself.

"*Aenti* Edith said she isn't coming today. She has chores to do. Who could it be?" M.J. asked. Since when had her youngest resorted to calling Edith her aunt? They clustered near the sitting room window and peered out. Two women climbed down from the buggy in matching blue dresses and white aprons. One was tall and shapely and younger than Hannah, the other short and maybe ten years her senior. They collected plates and a cake carrier from the buggy floor, then headed toward the house. Hannah straightened to the fact that she was about to face her first visitors.

"It looks like we're not going to the mill for

lunch today," she said, a bit disappointed. She hated that Daniel would be without his lunch, but she couldn't send the girls to deliver it by themselves, could she?

"Girls, remember, don't speak too much. Just smile, and be friendly." Hannah shot Catherine an extra look before nervously tidying her dress, apron and *kapp*. She couldn't remember the last time she'd cared so much about her looks, or how she'd fit in. She walked toward the front door, took a deep breath and opened it with a smile.

"Hello," Hannah said, stepping out, her daughters finding a place at her side. Their little hands primly gathered in front. To outsiders, they were adorable. To Hannah, they were really good at pretending.

"I'm Millie Troyer, your nearest neighbor, and this is Margaret Sayer. We've come to welcome you and your family to our community." Millie smiled, with a glint of sparkle in green eyes that contrasted boldly with her fair complexion.

"Please, come in." Hannah welcomed them inside. Thankfully, the kitchen was freshly cleaned, and the floors swept.

"I brought *kichlin*." Millie offered each girl a cookie from the plate in her hand before turning to Hannah. It tasted like bliss, with the warm chewy texture of cinnamon and molasses. Their local bakery back home had never made such delicious cookies like this.

"We feel terrible we only learned of your arrival today. Edith Schwartz isn't usually so secretive about newcomers, but Hazel Miller heard you moved in and married our sweet Daniel and told Eliza Lapp. She's a poor widow who lives just four or five farms from yours." Millie pointed south, juggled the plate still in her other hand. "Eliza isn't one for company, but Emma Byler, that's Hank Byler's *fraa*, she went to check in on her as she tends to do, and when Emma came by the orchard for a few melons from our garden, she told me all about it. I can't believe a week of days has come and gone and we didn't even know our Daniel found a *fraa* and brought her home to Miller's Creek," Millie said without taking a single breath.

Before replying, Hannah inhaled deeply, then said, "I'm sure Daniel was just giving us time to get settled." While Millie placed another cookie in her daughters' hands, Margaret strolled leisurely around the large kitchen. She ran a finger along the old hutch in the corner, her face pinched in disapproval. A bead of perspiration made a slow journey down between Hannah's shoulder blades. She mentally noted to add extra dusting to her list of duties. These women must think Daniel chose a lazy bride.

"Most marriages are performed with the community as witness," Margaret said, sounding doubtful.

"It was a simple, private ceremony," Hannah replied, earning her two quizzical looks from her visitors. She knew she should say as little as possible, knowing so little about Amish traditions still. Mentally, she ran through the facts she and Daniel had agreed upon, in case questions like this occurred.

"This pie looks *wunderbaar*," Hannah complimented Margaret, admiring the beautiful woman with ivory skin and pretty blond hair.

"Daniel is fond of my apple pie," Margaret said sharply. "I usually bring one by once a week, but was visiting family recently." Hannah almost gasped in surprise. Just as quick as Millie Troyer had made Hannah feel welcome with cookies and smiles, Margaret Sayer took it all back. It appeared that Margaret had only come to meet the woman who married Daniel, and found her unworthy. Feeling immediately insecure, Hannah put her partially eaten cookie down on the counter.

"I'm sure Hannah here knows Daniel's likes and dislikes well enough," Millie quickly chimed in. "What man doesn't live for a full belly and a clean house," she laughed. Hannah agreed, despite knowing those things didn't satisfy some men. Millie seemed kind enough, but the tension in the room was so thick you could cut it with a knife. As the girls took their cookies to the porch, Hannah put the kettle on for coffee. She'd finally figured out how to make a decent cup of coffee without the luxury of simply pushing a button.

"How did you and Daniel meet?" Margaret asked. Hannah turned from the stove, realizing that she was stubbornly sitting at the head of the kitchen table, in Daniel's chair, legs crossed with the upper one angrily swinging. "I speak to him nearly each week and he has never mentioned you to me before."

Everything suddenly became crystal clear. And Hannah felt a pang of guilt. Had she come between two sweethearts? This woman clearly had an interest in Daniel. She studied her cautiously. She was very pretty, frown and all. Had they been courting when Hannah and her girls were dropped on his doorstep? She and Daniel hadn't shared such information. Why hadn't Edith mentioned this to her before?

But one thing she knew for sure and certain—she had to stand firm, keep up the facade, for her children's sake. "He failed to mention your weekly conversations to me, as well," Hannah countered. "Daniel knew my late husband. After we lost him, I ran into Daniel and we… Well, how would one describe it?" She forced a bashful smile. "We connected rather well." It was only a small lie. Daniel knew nothing about Micah, except he'd put his family in danger, but they had come to grips with their roles. Hannah respected how he fulfilled his by playing dad to three little girls he had no connection to.

The screen door slammed and M.J. bounced in. Margaret didn't even flinch nor break eye contact with Hannah as her daughter toddled over to her.

"Oh, would you like another *kichli, liebling*?" Millie asked, handing her daughter another. "You are so sweet," Millie fussed.

"Danki." M.J. smiled. "I have a pet cow named Daisy." *Where did she learn that word?* Hannah wondered.

"Mudder, Rosemary needs you," Catherine said as she ran into the room. It was one thing for M.J. to try on the Amish words, but Catherine had been dead set against even wearing her prayer covering, though she was wearing it right now.

"Please excuse me for a moment." Hannah stepped out of the kitchen quickly and found her daughters all huddled in the sitting room. "What's wrong?"

"Nothing, we just thought you needed rescuing," Catherine said. "That one lady asks too many questions. She doesn't seem to like you, and you do still call us the wrong names sometimes." Hannah pulled her into a hug and smiled.

"You are a wonderful daughter." Hannah kissed her cheek. "Or should I say, *wunderbaar*? But we have to deal with this. I can't hide in here until they leave."

"We could try," Catherine said, quirking a grin. Oh, how Hannah had missed that grin. Suddenly, the front door opened again. Hannah hoped that more company hadn't decided to show up. She and her daughters stepped back into the kitchen just as Daniel rushed into the room, sweat pouring from his face. He looked as if he had run all the way from the mill. Hannah wasn't quite sure why he'd done so, but the soured expression on Margaret seemed to be part of it.

"*Daed*, we have visitors. Millie brought pie." M.J. beamed and started rocking heel to toe adorably. Hannah had managed to contain her shock from their visitors but not from Daniel, who was equally surprised at her youngest's growing vocabulary.

"Millie brought *kichlin* for the *kinner*. I brought the apple pie," Margaret corrected. "Your favorite. Should you not be at the mill at this hour?" Margaret tilted her head and smiled coyly. Hannah knew it wasn't right, feeling as if this stranger was making no effort to hide her thoughts, but she didn't like thinking this woman—who didn't know they weren't really married—was flirting with her husband.

"Both will be appreciated by all of us, *jah*?" Daniel slowed his breathing as Hannah crossed the room and fetched a glass from the cabinet so she could give him some water.

"*Mudder* makes pies too," Catherine added. "She makes the best pies." Daniel flinched, and she could tell he was already figuring out that things weren't going so well.

"I work next door, so it's easy enough to sneak in and see my family during the day," Daniel said. It wasn't a total lie, he could if he wanted to see in on them during the day. She filled a glass with water and handed it to him. As he drank, they both leaned against the counter, shoulder to shoulder. They were in this together.

"Sometimes *Mudder* takes lunch to him so they can have more time together," Catherine added. Hannah was shocked that Catherine came to his defense. Daniel drained his glass and she refilled it a second time. "We even packed a basket for him today." Catherine pointed out, grinning. Her daughter might look like her, but this one had Micah written all over her. The little trickster!

"Oh, we must have come at a bad time," Millie began before Margaret quickly added, "Will your Catherine be joining school soon? Lydia is a *wunderbaar* teacher and has a talent for…outspoken *kinner*." Margaret's gaze landed on Catherine briefly before returning to Daniel.

Hannah stiffened. No one was going to talk about her children like that. But before she could say anything, Daniel spoke. "We just married, and the *kinner* are adjusting to a new community and a new house. I'm sure you can understand how we are all trying to enjoy this special time together." Hannah was relieved, hearing all the reassurance in his voice. Millie and Margaret both had to believe this was a true marriage or Margaret would spread unwanted gossip. Margaret's frown began to deepen.

"*Jah*, of course. New couples need time to themselves," Millie agreed, looking to Margaret as if reminding her of her place. "I would love for your *dochdern* to come visit and perhaps have a sleepover with my three girls." All three girls' faces lit up. Was the idea of making friends here the reason for their excitement? "My Ivy is just about your Catherine's age. Though the other two are a wee bit older and they love *kinner*. Anytime you two want a moment to yourselves, let me know, *jah*?" Millie darted a knowing smile between Hannah and Daniel. Hannah felt her face turn hot. But she recovered quickly.

"Oh, that would be so appreciated, Millie. I still have so much to tend to around the house, but if that offer still stands in a couple of weeks, Daniel and I will definitely bring the girls over to visit. He's been so hard at work at the mill—" she touched his arm affectionately "—we haven't had much time together. I haven't even seen most the area and think a tour would be so lovely." When Hannah smiled up at Daniel a second time, he met her gaze with a smoldering look that steeled her. She had only meant to sound convincing, to pretend to be the happy newlyweds. The way those eyes were looking down on her, she was convinced that he was much better at pretending than she was.

"We should go and leave you all to your lunch."

"*Danki*, Millie, Margaret." Daniel nodded curtly. As Millie said farewell to the girls,

Hannah didn't miss the long look Margaret shot Daniel.

Feeling very much like a weed sprouting up between two perfectly constructed stepping stones, Hannah stepped away from Daniel.

"Let me walk you both out," she offered kindly. She guided both women out and thanked them again for the treats and the warm welcome. Following proper etiquette ingrained in her from a young age, Hannah invited them to visit again, though she wasn't sure Margaret would take her up on that offer.

It was the right thing to do, being kind to Daniel's neighbors. She waved goodbye and took a long breath before entering the kitchen again.

Daniel stood at the counter helping Catherine fill the lunch basket. She didn't move, just watched as the two worked silently together, each in their own thoughts. At the table, her youngest two children nibbled on cookies. It was a simple scene, yet, one she had never been privileged to witness before now. She probably shouldn't be thinking how sweet they all looked.

Like a regular family.

She couldn't ignore how Daniel rushed home to see them. He was a natural protector, a man who was meant to be head of a household. From the moment they met, he kept surprising her. Every encounter, every small talk shared between them, was having her craving the next one.

"Mommy, I pretended real good, didn't I?" M.J. called out and all eyes turned to her.

"Yes, you did, dear." Marshaling the thoughts swirling in her head, Hannah moved farther into the room.

"It seems I have a house filled with *schmaert maedels*." Daniel tossed her a wry grin.

"What's a *maedel*?"

"A young lady," Daniel answered, tapping her nose. It had become his show of affection to her little one.

"Are you a *maedel* too?" Hannah chuckled at her daughter's cookie-coated fingers and parade of questions. It had been a lot of years since she felt young.

"*Nee*, she is a *fraa*, a married woman," Daniel explained. While M.J. practiced the new word, Daniel leaned back on the counter, folded his arms and simply stared at Hannah. It was a bit intimidating and made her begin to feel terribly self-conscious. Was he angry with her acts of affection moments ago? Did he sense the tension between her and the woman he could have married and lived a perfectly normal life with?

In his unflinching stare, Hannah smoothed her palms down her dress and made a quick motion to assure her *kapp* was straight. "She is also a young *mudder*." His eyes perused her in full. Surely he was regretting this arrangement by now. The woman who left here just seconds ago was perfect.

"And possibly a great many other things I haven't discovered yet." Satisfied with his answers, M.J. resumed eating. Hannah on the other hand was shocked to the core. Less by his words than the intense look on Daniel's face. The churning in her belly stopped and was replaced with the soft flutters of attraction, affection and newness. She quickly placed a hand over her middle as if that alone would hide how he affected her.

It was then, in that fraction of a second, her words came back and strangled her. In answering Millie, Hannah had alluded to spending time with Daniel alone, seeing the area. Was he going to see she made good on those words? The very thought of long buggy rides across the valley or late evening strolls to the creek had her blood warming rapidly.

This time when their eyes collided, Daniel did smile and it didn't stop with his lips. It reached those hazel eyes until they smiled too. "It seems you can handle yourself just fine without me," he chuckled and gathered the basket on the counter. "I should get back to the mill before Eli puts up a fuss." He turned to the girls. "Don't be naming any more animals while I'm gone," he said playfully. Brushing past Hannah, he paused. "See you at supper, *fraa*." When the door shut, Hannah still hadn't moved.

Chapter Eight

Wednesday evening, Daniel walked home from the mill, clearing his head from the day's work and all the thoughts swirling in his head, using the time for prayer. It had always helped him before, when life got out of control. Now was one of those times. He was a husband and father in pretense only, but knowing it was all temporary, he had no idea how to take the helm. He wanted very much to love the girls freely. Provide them with stability, roots and a faith so strong they found healing just as he had. In short, they needed a father.

Then there was Hannah. When she looked at him and smiled yesterday, he couldn't help that his heart hammered, in fact he'd been defense-less against it. Her delicate beauty pulled him in. The way her eyes smiled at her daughters even when her mouth didn't move. It didn't go unnoticed how fast she had taken to his life, his world. The woman was determined to master anything and everything put in front of her. It caught him off guard, these feelings. He was a lonely man. And this was Michael's wife, an *Englisher* and a city dweller. But when he looked at her, he didn't see who she was before. Daniel saw Hannah, the Plain-dressed and protective mother with honey blond hair and eyes that made a man question everything. He'd never expected to be drawn to her when he agreed to this, but her air of fragility raised his protectiveness, and her eyes awakened his heart.

"*Gott*, don't let me get used to this. If You are going to take them away, make it swift," he prayed heavenward. He was not near as strong as he thought he was.

"Now you stop being nasty." Daniel heard the little voice as he closed the pasture gate and reached the yard.

M.J. stood in her new green dress, barefoot, pointing a crooked stick at his cantankerous rooster. "Trying to make friends with chickens now?" he teased. She turned toward him and beamed a little sunshine his way. It had been a long day, with orders piling up faster than he could cut them, and Bates had called to inform him of the current status of Corsetti, which was still undetermined. Coming home to her smiling face was just what he needed.

"*Hinkel. Aenti* Edith says it's not a chicken, but a *hinkel*." She shrugged adorably. "This one tries to bite Mommy every time she wants to get the eggs. I'm going to train him." Daniel wondered when she had started referring to Edith that way, then shook off the thought. Martha Jane was a wonder, fearless and social, and hoping to train a chicken to obey commands. Did his brother ever know how blessed he was?

"Even little Amish girls call them chickens, and for your information, that big fellow is a rooster. If he thinks you're afraid of him, he will take advantage."

She scrunched her little face. "*Nee*, I'm not afraid." She demonstrated by pushing her shoulders back and walking right up to the red rooster with colorful tail plumage. "Go back to bed until you can be nice to *Mudder*," she ordered, shaking her measly stick at him. Daniel stepped closer to intervene in case the old rooster had had enough, but suddenly found himself in awe when the rooster turned and stalked straight into the henhouse.

"How did you do that?"

"I dunno." She shrugged. "Maybe he is afraid of me." Daniel laughed so hard he thought he might start crying. "I made you happy," she added. "I like it!"

"*Jah*, you made me happy, and I like it too." If only all of life's troubles could be so easily cured with M.J.'s smiles and crooked sticks. "How was everyone today?"

"Catherine said I'm not allowed to call you *Daed*, since we already had one." She tapped her finger to her chin as if she were thinking. "*Mudder* was invited to a sewing party or sister party. I dunno what that is. She doesn't have sisters she said and looked sad. I don't think she wants to go. And Roslyn hasn't cried all day." Daniel appreciated the full report of the house.

"Sister's Day. That's sort of like sewing bees and frolics where the women of the community get together and quilt, or can food, or bake lots of sweets. It's a way of helping each other and taking care of everyone's needs."

"*Daed*, is there milking frolics too?" M.J. asked. The girl was taken with cows, that was for sure and certain.

"*Nee*, no milking frolics, I'm afraid. And you don't have to call me *Daed*. You can just call me Daniel."

"*Aenti* Edith taught me. It's how you say *daddy* in Amish. I am an Amish girl now, you know." Her face scrunched adorably. Powerless against her charm, Daniel lifted her off the ground and gave her a tickle.

"You laugh like one too," he jested as he carried her into the house.

Hannah had made a spicy rice dish with sausage for dinner. Daniel had never heard of it, but found it to his liking. The spices warmed his bones against the early October chill and cleared the sinuses. He was on his second helping when Hannah asked, "So Millie and Margaret mentioned sending the girls to school."

"I'm not going to an Amish school, Mom," Catherine said. "They probably don't even use real books."

"They do use real books, Catherine. And most Amish children are needed at home, so they have to learn everything *Englisch* kids do, but faster."

"Faster? What does that mean?" Catherine asked.

Daniel froze mid-bite at her sudden attention. He detected eagerness in the face of a challenge in this one and mentally stored the information away. He had noted little things about each of them. They all had their own different personalities. Rosemary trembled more at night than during the day, but she had jumped in to help her mother with household duties. M.J. liked reminding the world to smile, and making friends, even if they were angry roosters. She was eager to fit in, much like her mother, Daniel quietly assessed. Hannah wanted to fit in, and make everyone happy. Daniel could see that all the changes to her life were taking their toll on her. There was a weariness in her eyes. Common house noises made her stiffen, and he had a feeling she wasn't sleeping at night. He wished he knew how to ease her worries. But like with Catherine, he might have just found a way in.

"*Jah*, Amish children only go to school until eighth grade. They pass the same tests to do so as seniors do in *Englisch* high schools." Catherine crossed her arms over her chest, indicating she didn't believe him. "I think school is a *gut* idea. You all could make friends your own age, and I bet you'd learn faster than the other kids your age. It would be *gut* not to get behind in your lessons too." Daniel forked another bite of rice into his mouth and watched as Catherine's mind processed everything he'd said.

By the end of the meal, Daniel was certain Catherine would understand the importance of going to the local school. Standing, she collected her plate and turned to her mother. "Please don't make me go to an Amish school."

If he was going to get this one to comply to

what was normal in his world, he would have to find another way to do it.

Like most evenings, Hannah followed Daniel to the porch after supper was cleared from the table. It was the only time they could speak without little ears about. "I can't force her to go to school here if she doesn't want to, Daniel. That wasn't part of the deal."

"It will be *gut* for her. I'll drive her myself and pick her up. It's normal, and normal is *gut, jah?*"

"She'll be angry we're making her go, and she'll be impossible to live with." Hannah didn't need the aggravation.

"Then blame me. Tell her I insist that she goes," he said gruffly. Hannah could tell he was still put off with her since Millie and Margaret had visited. Did he wish Margaret were here with him talking about sending children to school instead of her?

"I'm sorry I let my mouth run off like it did when Millie and Margaret visited that day. I didn't mean to come between you and Margaret. I was only trying to make this look real."

"I'm sorry too." She looked in his eyes, trying to read his thoughts, but to no avail.

"You didn't have to rush over here, you

know. I can handle a few visitors from the community, including your girlfriend."

"*Nee*, I rushed over because you shouldn't be alone. I promised to help you and that includes dealing with people you don't know." And the price he was paying was too much. Her and the girls being here had cost him the chance for a real family of his own. For a long moment, she saw him for the decent man he was. He was a rare and wonderful human being. How many men would have gone to the same lengths he had for mere strangers? "And she is *not* my girlfriend."

Hannah stiffened. "When a woman bakes you pies weekly, she wants to be." Did he think her blind?

Daniel took a step closer. Close enough she could smell the scent of sawdust and sweat that penetrated his clothing.

"Married men don't have girlfriends," he said in a low tone.

"Some do." She quickly averted her gaze, regretting the slip of the tongue immediately. "She is very pretty and clearly cares for you."

"Does that bother you?" he queried.

She looked up at him; those hazel eyes searching her for an answer were making her breathless. He was forcing her entire world to shift. "Yes, it bothers me. You've wasted your chance at a real wife by helping us. I'm not heartless, Daniel. We've disrupted your life, maybe even ruined it. Edith told me the truth, that we likely can't get an annulment when this is over. That we will have to stay married. We owe you so much for letting us be here…"

"My help is freely given. Maybe my life needed disrupting, and I have a real wife, however short-lived. I had a choice. We all have a choice. Nothing is ruined, Hannah." She couldn't believe that. She had taken advantage, spoiled his future, and he was making it sound as if she had not burdened him in any way.

"What about when we leave? This isn't our home. We will leave, eventually, Daniel. What about your future? My decision to agree to come here has taken that from you." She felt the first sting of tears threaten.

"Our future is in *Gott*'s hands. You are not that powerful, *liewe*." He grinned down at her. "And this is our home."

"You're not angry with me, are you?" She looked up, confused. Micah would have stirred up such a fuss at her boldness in front of others.

"*Nee*, I could never be angry with you. I'm committed to this. I care for your *dochdern*, I can't lie about that." Then she saw it. For just a second, she saw him, truly saw him. She had been missing all the signs right in front of her. Daniel was not the kind of man who lied to get what he wanted. But what was it he wanted? She took a step back, and reined in her common sense.

He cared for her girls, possibly loved them. He wanted what Micah never did. Daniel wanted children.

Hannah suspected he would sacrifice more for her daughters' sakes if asked. The quicker she understood that the better.

Her heart was in danger and she knew it. A woman would be a fool not to see what stood in front of her. Daniel Raber was a man to measure all men by.

"Micah didn't do that." The words slipped before she could stop them.

"What do you mean?" he asked.

"He never cared about something besides his job. Here you are, a stranger, sacrificing your entire future for us. I would understand if you want us to leave, to go someplace else." Daniel shook his head as if leaving wasn't an option.

"No place will be safer for you, for them, than here with me." Why was it so hard to breathe hearing him say that, to have him so close? They stood and stared at one another in a silence thick with choices, possibilities and regrets. She worried if they stood there much longer, she would make a fool of herself with him. Reveal her feelings. He was struggling too, some inner battle she wasn't privy to. As if only now noticing how close he was hovering over her, Daniel took two steps back.

"Catherine should start attending school next week. And it would be *gut* to have Rosemary helping with the animals. She's made for it. And…" He paused, grinned at the thought. "Let's have M.J. gather the eggs from now on."

Hannah was surprised by his demands that weren't actually very demanding. "But that rooster…" Daniel tossed her a smirk as he made his way down the porch steps, and then turned to face her again.

"She can handle him, trust me. That one is the least of your concerns. I have a couple big orders this week, but after I think it's a *gut* time you learned to drive a buggy."

"I can't…" she started to protest.

"You can. You will take that to task too," Daniel said as he walked away from her.

Hannah stood on the porch and watched him go check on the animals, making his nightly rounds and see that all was as it should be before getting to bed. Daniel always had the same routine. A woman could set her watch by what time he woke each morning, milked the cow, went to work at the mill, returned home and walked over his farm to see no killers lurked about. Did he ever do anything spontaneous? She hoped not. Very few things in her life had ever been predictable, and Hannah found she suddenly liked predictable.

And hazel eyes.

Chapter Nine

Hannah triple-checked each daughter to make sure they were ready. Their *kapps* were stiff and white, their dresses ironed and even their new shoes shined, though Edith didn't press on doing so. If anyone in Miller's Creek mistook them for *Englisch* today, it would be for whatever poured out of one of her daughters' mouths, not for how they looked.

"Now, remember. Talk as little as possible, and don't use the Amish words Edith has been teaching you unless you feel comfortable with them." Hannah had been reluctant to try them herself, but M.J. thought each new word Edith taught her was more fascinating than the next. "Okay, Rosemary?" Hannah was only rewarded with a headshake. What Hannah wouldn't give to hear Rosemary mutter the simplest sound. Her silence was said to be temporary, but living on the road, hiding from a killer, was supposed to be temporary too, and here it was nearly three weeks later and temporary was still their lives. Hannah had decided today, as they planned on joining the community for church services, that temporary could deal with itself.

"What if someone doesn't think I'm an Amish girl?" M.J. asked.

"Just say we are from Indiana and that's how we talk." *Simple as that*, Hannah thought.

"Is that a lie? *Daed* says not to lie." M.J.'s face scrunched.

"He is not our dad," Catherine snapped. "Mom, make her stop calling him that." Hannah exhaled.

"M.J., you don't have to call Daniel Dad." Hannah reminded her a second time.

"But *Aenti* Edith says you are married so he is my *daed*. Mine is gone. Don't you want me to have one?" Hannah was speechless. How did one tell a five-year-old it was all pretend? Hannah and Catherine locked eyes. Even she had no quick reply right now.

"What I do want is for us to get going. We don't want to be late for church. We can talk about this later," Hannah stated as she ushered them out of the shared bedroom. It would be the first time any of them rode in a buggy, the first time going to an Amish church and the first time they would have to present themselves as a family in public. That was enough firsts to deal with for one day. Her nerves frayed, her stomach in knots, and even though the house held a slight chill this October morning, Hannah found herself perspiring.

Outside, Daniel lifted each girl into the buggy and instructed them to sit in the back, M.J. in the center, her sisters on each side, then held out a hand to Hannah.

"You don't need to help me, Daniel. I can do it," she insisted, putting her foot to the high step.

"I have no doubt, but humor me." Daniel grinned, taking her hand in his. As much as she hated to admit it, he did in fact make the climb easier. It was his warm, calloused hands that was hard to ignore. There was no way Daniel could be allowed to spark anything in her. Bryan would find Corsetti and then they'd soon return to the real world. *It's all just pretend*, she reminded herself.

At the sound of Daniel clicking his tongue, the horse jerked forward and the buggy began to move. Hannah looked over her shoulder to see that her girls weren't frightened in the least. Surprisingly even Catherine looked entertained. She had to admit, she too felt the air of excitement as the horse picked up speed.

"Just enjoy the ride," Daniel whispered to her. "It is a slower pace than you are used to traveling, for sure and certain." He smirked. "But slowing down has its own rewards."

As soon as they pulled onto the blacktop of the road, Hannah took in the passing scenery as she felt the slight jerks and pulls of the buggy. Watching Colt stretch and move was making her nauseous. She pulled her eyes away, looked at the driver again. Daniel was trusting their lives to the hooves of an animal. She forced herself to focus on the scenery again and not the scenarios playing in her mind.

Leaves had lost their lush emeralds and had traded them for bold reds, bright oranges, and a yellow that Hannah could only describe as mellow and earthy. Barns towered over homes, and homes were few and far between. Land rolled gently, pastures fenced in a backdrop of forest. How had she lived so long and not seen such beauty in person?

Hannah took special care to note all the mums and sunflowers lining walkways and lingering in gardens that looked barren elsewise. She had picked vegetables in Daniel's garden, learned how to can tomatoes thanks to

Edith, but wondered what it would feel like to touch virgin soil, plant a seed, watch it grow. In his world, such a thing wasn't just a metaphor. All her life, she'd rushed from one thing to the next. What would it be like to slow down, enjoy the fruits of your labors? When she realized Daniel had been watching her, Hannah jerked back to reality.

"You look nice," he said, then faced the road again. "Are you nervous?"

Hannah glanced down at the new dress Edith had sewn for her. The rose-colored hue complemented her hair and skin rather nicely. Maybe she needed to learn how to sew. It wasn't right that Edith was teaching her so many things about life on an Amish farm, and she was making her and her daughters clothes too.

"A little," she admitted. "How far is the church?" She brushed her hands over her lap.

"We don't have a church building like the *Englisch* do. I thought Edith would have explained it to you." Giggles sounded behind them, and Daniel turned to cast a smile at her daughters in the back seat. They were enjoying the ride, and it couldn't be ignored how they were thriving here. It was all Daniel's doing. Daniel made a good father. His patience, the way he watched them when he thought no one was looking, and how he knew how to approach each one differently. She glanced over to him as he controlled the reins. Though he had suddenly stopped shaving, he looked fresh, crisp in his newly pressed shirt and jacket.

"We have services every other Sunday. Each family takes turns holding the service and the fellowship meal that follows in their home, or barn, whichever has the most room. Today, we are going to Sayer's farm. Bennie Sayer and his wife usually have services inside their home, and when weather is nice like today, the meal is eaten outside."

Hannah tensed immediately. "I didn't make anything. Why didn't you tell me there was a fellowship meal? Daniel, how can I show up empty-handed?" She was furious no one mentioned such an important detail until now. Even worse, he was smiling about it.

"You have just moved into a new home, with three children and a new husband. But if it makes you feel better, Edith made two peanut butter pies and a plate of cookies this morning while you were all sleeping late, again." He chuckled. "They are in the back of the buggy."

"You find this funny, don't you?" Hannah couldn't help but find herself drawn to him and his genial mood. Was it normal to find him so appealing when he was nothing like the man she had married? Then again, maybe that was what attracted her even more. Daniel was nothing like Micah at all.

"I do," he replied playfully. The beginnings of his beard gave him a more rugged look that Hannah found quite appealing. "But to keep you from being angry with me all day, I will tell you also that most of the service isn't in English. The service will last about three hours. Men sit on one side of the room, and women on the other."

"Anything else I should know?" How was Hannah supposed to convince three children to sit still for that long?

"Along with the other women, you will help serve the meal. Men eat first, then women and children." He turned the buggy down a long gravel road and she watched the tension in his jaw work.

Was he holding something back? "What else are you not telling me?"

"Nothing. The community is filled with wonderful people and you might just enjoy yourself." Hannah shot him a disapproving frown though she secretly had to admit she was looking forward to seeing Millie again. "While you're here, you might as well enjoy it," he added.

When they pulled up to a smaller barn filled

with tables, Daniel helped each of them down and placed a dessert in the children's hands. He said something in Amish to a younger man who led the horse and buggy around back. Hannah felt her hands start to tremble as she took in the scene. The lawn was crowded with people, many of them going in and out of the house and barn. A horse nickered nearby and she jerked, a faint sound escaping her throat. On impulse, Daniel reached for her hand.

"I will be with you, for now," Daniel said as he began leading her forward.

Hannah thought she might just be sick. There was over a hundred people here, and so far no Edith to guide her. Daniel had been kind to take her hand. In fact, she was surprisingly calm knowing he was taking control. For once, she didn't mind someone else was leading.

Daniel was right about one thing: sitting three hours on a backless wooden bench, listening to words in a language you didn't understand was exhausting. Hannah was proud of the girls for sitting still through it all. Even M.J. managed not to squirm or ask for the bathroom. It was proof they were all trying. Rosemary was skittish, but as soon as the women gathered in the kitchen to help put out food and drinks, her daughter was eager to be helpful.

"Does she not speak?" Hannah heard one woman whisper to another as Edith instructed Hannah to carry pies to the table just under the porch canopy. Another woman responded in a different language, and Hannah had no clue what she was saying. She promised herself she would try to learn more of the German dialect Edith called *Deitch*, though she made mention that here in the northern tip of the state, their language was very different from communities farther north. No matter what language, or version thereof, Hannah hated not knowing if she and her children were being gossiped about right in front of her.

"*Nee*, she is just very shy, but her sister makes up for her silence." Edith called out to M.J. and Hannah watched her daughter skip over, and start a full conversation about Daisy the cow and Marigold, the newest name she had concocted for one of Daniel's pesky goats, to the group of women who had been placing covered food dishes on an adjacent table.

Edith caught her attention then. "Hannah, this is Hazel Miller, she lives just a few miles from you." Hannah set down an apple pie on the table and brushed her palms on her apron before turning her attention to Hazel. She was a bit taller than Hannah. Fanned out wrinkles around her eyes suggested she might be in her fifties, but her skin glowed as fresh as a teenager's, unblemished and perfect.

"We heard our Daniel up and married an old sweetheart and thought we were being fed untruths. But I can see you are very much real, and such a *schee fraa* you are. I met your *kinner*. They are sweet." Hazel put her hands on her full hips and smiled welcomingly. Hannah quickly spied each daughter to note her whereabouts before answering.

"*Danki*. They can be sweet…in public," Hannah replied. The comment earned her a few innocent chuckles. She needed to talk with Daniel and decide how to handle these kinds of questions.

"Well, we were blessed when Daniel returned to us, and now even more blessed to have you and your *kinner* in our community too. I run the bakery in town. You should come by for *kaffi* and a scone someday," Hazel offered kindly.

"How kind of you," Hannah replied, wishing she could. No doubt, law enforcement was closing in on Corsetti, and time for drinking coffee and eating scones with Hazel was growing slim. It was too bad though, because Hazel reminded her of her foster mother, Anna, so much. Sitting for an hour with her would be a welcome respite to this unusual life she suddenly found herself living.

"*Wie geht's*, I'm Sara Plank. My Eli works for your Daniel." Sara was tall, thin and had the most beautiful green eyes Hannah had ever seen. She looked nothing like Hannah would have she imagined when Daniel spoke of his boisterous foreman.

"Nice to meet you." Hannah hoped her lack of Amish wasn't noticeable. She knew so few words but wasn't that confident in using them.

"That littlest one over there—" Sara pointed to three boys chasing grasshoppers in the nearby brittle grass, "—is Jesse. He is about the age of your Catherine, *jah*? The other two are his best friends." Sara chuckled in a motherly tone. "Can't keep them apart." Hannah watched the boys cluster together, comparing their catches, and laughed.

"So where did you say you were from, Hannah?" Margaret suddenly appeared in the growing cluster of women. Hannah was the new mysterious bride in their midst. She felt her stomach start to roll, never liking to be the center of attention. If the women weren't already suspicious of her being here, Margaret would raise enough questions to warrant them to be. She knew jealousy was sin, but seeing Margaret dressed in a periwinkle blue that accentuated all her finer qualities made Hannah feel like a wren among cardinals.

Across the yard, where a large huddle of men were standing in the open barn doorway, Hannah locked eyes with Daniel. He had been watching her get acquainted. She didn't need rescuing. Surely, she could handle a few Amish women after handling some of the nitpicky clients she had endured in the past. So why did she feel so small, unworthy of their friendship? Then he smiled. It was just what she needed to gain her footing.

"We lived in Indiana. I believe I mentioned that when you brought over Daniel's favorite pie to the house the other day." Margaret's eyes narrowed. Even here, women had boundaries and Hannah was marking hers. Daniel said Margaret meant nothing to him, and she hoped that was the truth, because the last thing that she needed was a jaded sweetheart asking too many questions and stirring up trouble, trouble that could cost her children their lives. "It was very…*gut*," Hannah added.

"But Daniel lived in Chicago before coming home. How did you two meet?" Margaret continued to prod. Hannah struggled for an answer. Had Daniel lived long outside the Amish?

"Now, Margaret, let's not overwhelm her

with such personal questions," Millie intruded. Hannah knew she liked Millie Troyer. "Hannah, you make sure to try the triple-berry pie." Millie pointed to the table of desserts. "Frances Byler makes it and it's the finest in the county." Millie looked beautiful in her teal dress.

"I was just curious about the kind of community she came from. If they are so different than our own, that's all," Margaret defended, looking as innocent as a tulip blossom. Hannah saw past the fresh ivory skin and rosy lips. Margaret was a pit bull, refusing to let go.

"I haven't been here long enough to answer that, but I can't imagine them being too different. Bishop Schwartz was very welcoming, and Edith…" Hannah smiled her way "…she's been so kind helping me and my daughters get the house in order." Hannah took a careful breath.

"It's our way to help one another, ain't so? We're so thrilled to have you here with us," Millie said warmly, shooting Margaret a warning glare.

"Well, I'm glad you and Daniel reconnected. You make a fine match," Hazel added.

"Hazel here is known for her matchmaking in our community," Edith informed, looping a hand around Hazel's arm in sisterly fashion.

"Seventeen couples and counting," Hazel replied proudly. "I did worry Daniel would never settle down. Didn't know his heart had been taken by an Amish *maedel* even when he lived among the *Englisch*. I'm just glad he came back to us, and suspect you had some influence in that." Hazel winked. "We all have much to thank you for." Hannah was speechless. These women thought she was the reason Daniel was back with the Amish. It sounded like his time in the English world was longer than a few short *rumspringa* years.

"I hate to lose one of our own to the *Englisch* world. I still can't get over why Dan Raber ran off like he did, taking our sweet Martha Jane and the *buwe* with her." Hannah cocked a brow but didn't dare pry Sara for details. That would make her look like she didn't know her own husband, exposing her for the liar she was.

It would explain why Daniel's accent wasn't as thick as everyone else's. Had that been why Bryan insisted she stay here? Did Daniel have a long enough history in her world that made him more inclined to help her family fit in to this one?

"Oh, now Michael, he was a handful, always running off and playing pranks on others," Hazel said.

"And stealing every *kichli* he could get his hands on," Millie added, earning her numerous head nods.

"Not Daniel. He was nothing like his *bruder*," Hazel added. *Brother?* Hannah stopped for a second, then busied herself cutting pies as she listened to the ladies talk about Daniel and his family.

"Oh, Margaret, please go fetch the dessert plates. We can't make Hannah do all the work," Hazel ordered, and Hannah almost chuckled aloud when Margaret's frown deepened.

"Don't mind her, Hannah. Margaret is just upset you snagged him first," Millie said, patting her arm. "Now, how are you adjusting, dear?"

Hannah wished she could tell them the truth: *Oh, I'm a fake widow named Magnolia who is ruining a man's one chance at love and family to keep my children safe from a killer. And oh, by the way, my real husband was a stranger to me too, secretly stealing money from mobsters and pretending to uphold the law.* Hannah hated lies, and she was lying to these wonderful women who had shown her nothing but kindness, and who made her feel as if she were one of them. She hoped God would forgive her.

"The girls are adjusting well. Rosemary is still a little shaken from all the changes but as you can see…" All eyes followed her gaze to M.J., now in Daniel's arms, telling a group of bearded men some tale that was earning their full attention. "That one has never met a stranger."

"He looks like a natural. I think our Daniel has finally found his place," Hazel said behind her. "You have given him what he needed most." Hannah scrutinized Daniel's well-proportioned frame and wavy dark hair peeking from beneath his straw hat. The way he held M.J., he looked like a father, smiling proudly as she entertained Daniel's friends. Hannah had to admit, regardless of how hard it was, anyone who didn't know them would think the two belonged together. M.J. would be heartbroken when they had to leave eventually. Daniel hung the stars in her eyes.

"You are young yet, maybe there will be *sohns* for him also," Sara chimed in. Hannah quickly hid her shock in a series of coughs.

"*Ach*, let's not put her on the spot now." Edith tapped Hannah's back but her wide smile said she liked Sara's way of thinking.

"Oh, and remember, I have an orchard. How about I bring over apples next week and we can start on pies and maybe teach the *kinner* to can pie filling and sauce for winter? Then you can tell me all about how Daniel asked you to marry him. I have always loved to hear such stories," Millie said, clutching her chest.

Hannah nodded. A day with Millie would be delightful, but chatting about romantic moments that didn't exist, not so much. The women were too kind, complimenting her and thinking her better than she was. How would they feel about her after…she left him? How would Daniel be looked at when his wife and children disappeared?

Hannah took a long, slow breath, calming her turbulent insides. She was making friends and falling in love with a world made of second hand comforts, but it was all a lie. They weren't the perfect family. Daniel wasn't her husband. He didn't love them.

He couldn't love her.

Chapter Ten

"So, you managed to get a *fraa* and *kinner* in one day without your community even knowing?" Daniel stiffened as Bennie Sayer strolled up beside them. He sat M.J. down, and instructed her to go find her mother. As soon as her little chubby legs disappeared around the corner, he addressed Bennie.

"You know full well I have never done anything halfway," Daniel chuckled lightheartedly. "How is your *mudder*? I heard she has been feeling poorly and didn't see her in attendance today." Daniel knew Margaret's father had only stomped over to find out why he had married a stranger and not his persistent daughter. A distraction was in order.

"Her heart condition has been giving her bouts of troubles lately," Bennie said, as he stood in front of him, feet set apart, gray eyes narrowing toward Daniel.

"We will continue to keep her in our prayers," Joshua said, untwisting a butterscotch candy wrapper and popping the candy into his mouth.

"Margaret has been most helpful. She cooks and cleans for her, and never complains. She's a *maedel* who knows what is important, *jah*?" Bennie's gaze remained on Daniel.

Daniel remained silent, and by the grace of *Gott*'s good timing, a voice called out, signaling the start of the fellowship meal so he didn't have to respond.

Daniel sat between Eli Plank and Vernon Schwartz at one of the long tables. In the distance, he saw M.J. playing with other children. Daniel watched closely when Aiden Shetler joined in. Ben and Barb's son was always finding himself in the middle of trouble and his M.J. needed no encouragement.

Rosemary, wearing the same blue hue as Millie, stood close by their neighbor at the desserts table as Hannah served ice water to men who were already seated. There was no sign of Catherine, but just as Daniel was about to excuse himself to seek her out, she appeared with Edith herding her toward the house. Whatever disturbance she had tried to muster, Edith was dealing with it so Hannah didn't have to. The woman had her hands full enough. Losing her husband and living in a strange place, all while learning a whole new way of life with three children. It was admirable how easy she had adapted. He had never met a woman who carried such a load and yet, as he watched her smile, working down the table, she made everything look easy. As if she belonged. He wished he weren't so attracted to her, but what man with two good eyes wouldn't be? She was small and dainty, could wrangle five-year-olds and pestering goats, and he noticed yesterday just how fast she could outrun an angry rooster too. She had known suffering in her life, and yet never complained. She didn't tire easily, and was a natural-born giver. The qualities he had always sought out in a possible wife.

"Water?" Hannah appeared at his side. She didn't look at him. Instead, she nervously looked to see how many eyes were watching them. He owed her for the remark to Millie, about letting the girls have a sleepover so they could spend time alone. Even though they both were pretending, Daniel couldn't resist making her blush for making him wonder what spending time alone with her would be like. He reached up as she poured his glass and touched her upper arm affectionately and smiled, just as any appreciative husband would have. It all backfired when she met his gaze. Daniel was dumbstruck. How could such a look of surprise, of vulnerable innocence, affect him so strongly? Hannah jerked, leaving a small splash of water on his arm, and hurried away. His instincts were fairly sound. She'd felt that too.

"You got stars in your eyes." Eli nudged him.

"*Jah*, I guess I do."

October was upon them. Days were warm. Nights ran chilly. Hannah let the cool breeze wash over her as they aimed their buggy toward home.

"That was interesting," Hannah said as the girls drifted to sleep behind them on the buggy ride home. Their bellies were full and they were worn out from playing.

"Was the service difficult to follow?"

"My High German is as good as my Pennsylvania Dutch," she teased him.

"*Ach*, well, when you learn one, you will learn the other." He'd said *when*. Had he meant to? Daniel was very careful with his words.

"You never told me you were raised in Chicago. Is that why Bryan thought this was such a good idea, because you once lived outside the Amish faith?" Daniel stiffened.

"Perhaps," Daniel replied. He wasn't going to make this easy on her, but Hannah knew how to be persistent.

"So what made you want to return and join the church?"

"I was born in the community, Hannah. But my father was unhappy here, and moved us away when I was young. I'm surprised anyone mentioned it. Feels like a very long time ago." He gave the horse a tap, and Colt responded, picking up the pace.

Hannah could sense that he didn't want to talk about his family or his time living in Chicago. "It's just that…you know a lot about me, that I grew up in foster homes, lost a husband and now I'm hiding out in the middle of nowhere with you. But I had to find out from strangers who you are." What was he afraid she would find out? "They believe I am an old girlfriend you just happened to run into. They think we have a history together."

"Edith must have spread that information."

"Well, spill it, mister. I can't act like your wife if every bit of news about you is a surprise to me."

"I lived in Chicago a long time ago, *jah*, but

now I'm back here where I belong. There is nothing secretive about it," Daniel said prickly.

When he brought the buggy to a stop in the drive, Hannah stepped down with ease. Nudging Catherine awake, she helped her eldest from the buggy before fetching M.J. and cradling her sleepy daughter against her Without a word, Daniel lifted Rosemary to his shoulder as he and Hannah glared at one another.

"I'm going to my room," Catherine muttered as Hannah and Daniel moved through the foyer and headed toward the sitting room. They placed the two sleepy girls on opposite ends of the couch.

"She has a room?"

"Did you not say she could have one?"

"I thought they were still sleeping with you. I'm glad one of you is comfortable enough here," he whispered in a snarky tone before heading out the door. Hannah followed. No way was he going to act mad at her when she was the one who was angry.

"I'm not the only one who isn't comfortable. Who's Michael?" Hannah demanded.

Daniel stopped in his tracks. "We aren't talking about this now, Hannah. I agreed to offer you and your *dochdern* a safe place, food and shelter. But my life before you is none of your business." Daniel stormed off to the barn, leaving her with more questions than answers.

Hannah's life had taken some sharp detours at times, but right now it was Daniel Raber's side roads she was concerned about. How could she trust someone who couldn't be honest with her? Why was he being secretive with her all of a sudden?

Long after the skies grew dark and the children were tucked into their beds, Daniel still hadn't returned to the house. Hannah paced the kitchen floor like a nervous hen. Thunder boomed in the distance, jolting her already frayed nerves. Something scraped the sitting room windows; the barren rose bush she thought, but the eerie creaks and groans heightened her senses. It was an old house, she told herself, shifting and settling, searching for a comfy spot to wait out a storm. It had been a good many years since she felt alone, but tonight she felt more isolated than ever. She wanted Daniel to come inside, bring that sense of safety back into the house. She wanted answers to her many questions, but if he would just come in, she wouldn't address them tonight. She would just be thankful he returned and that would be that.

Her heart thudded to a stop when she heard the sound of boots on the porch outside. For a second, she played out the dreaded scenario. What if Corsetti had found them? What if he had found Daniel brooding in the barn, and now had come to kill her children? She backed against the counter, searched out anything she could use as a weapon when the door creaked open, then closed.

The lock clicked into place as it routinely did and her wild imagination vanished in an exhaled breath.

In the dark foyer, Daniel's tall silhouette stood. He removed his hat, hung it carefully on the third peg as always and removed his boots before stepping into the kitchen. When their eyes locked, Hannah could see the color drain from his face.

"You should be resting," he said in a deep tone as he moved to the sink and washed his hands. "Staying up every night, waiting for something bad to happen isn't healthy."

"I don't like this arrangement any more than you, but you did agree to it," she blurted out.

"*Jah*, I agreed to help you, but there are some things I can't share with you, Hannah. Not right now," he said firmly. Was there any man more confusing than Daniel Raber? She thought not.

"How can I trust a man I don't know with my children? M.J. is growing attached to you.

Before church today, you promised them an adventure in order to get them to behave. You bribed them."

"It worked, didn't it?"

"And you let her name the cow and a goat. Can't you see how this is a problem? We don't know you." She backed up into the hutch. Dishes rattled but none fell.

"Do you want me to stop being kind to your children? Do you want me to stay distant, only protecting them from afar?" He pinned her with a look that could scare scales off fish.

"This was a mistake. This was all a big mistake. What have I done? Why did Micah do this to us? None of this should be happening." She dropped into a chair and began to sob. Daniel slowly crossed the floor and pulled out the seat beside her.

"You miss him. I'm sorry you have to go through this." Hannah's head snapped up. And she looked at him.

"One minute, life was good. My girls were happy and I had a job that wasn't too bad. Then I blinked and a cop was whisking me away, my children were inconsolable and Micah was dead. I blinked and here we are, wearing *kapps* and baking applesauce. I have no idea what I'm doing." Daniel leaned forward and took both her shaking hands.

"Neither do I, but if anyone can do this, it is you." Hannah looked at him as if he were speaking a different language. "We will both just practice not blinking so much," he said, letting go of her hands.

He was silent for a long moment, then said softly, "They were killed." Hannah looked at the man she thought could handle anything, his shoulders slumped, his head low.

"I'm sorry."

His heart couldn't take seeing Hannah in tears. She missed her husband, the life they shared, and here he was making things harder for her. It would be painful, the past usually was, but he had to give her something.

"My parents, they owned a store and it was robbed. The man only got two-hundred-and-nine dollars and killed them because he could."

"I… I shouldn't have…"

"No, you were right," Daniel admitted. He wanted to tell her the truth, but now was not the time. Marshal Bates was right about that. It was clear Hannah had suffered a lot in such a short time. Adding more salt to her wounds would be the wrong move. "We will pray, get some rest and face the next day. Then we will do that the next day and the next, for as long as it takes. Then you can go back to your real life." Did she still want that? *Stupid*. Of course, she wanted the life she was accustomed to. Freedoms his world didn't allow for.

"Real life. I don't think I even know what's real anymore," she scoffed. He lifted a hand, thumbed away a lonely tear sliding down her cheek.

"I don't have all the answers, but just remember you aren't alone." And she and the children never would be again, he promised himself. "I know it's not the same. I am not your husband in your heart. I know this has been difficult and you miss him."

She looked up under long, damp lashes. "I don't miss him," she confessed, more tears deciding to run south. "You probably think me a horrible person for saying that. But he became someone I didn't know anymore."

"I'm sure he loved you, despite the mess he got himself into." Daniel believed that. Michael would have never married her if he didn't love her. Hannah was so easy to love.

"In the beginning, he loved me, but then he just…stopped. I don't know why, not really." She shook her head. "I'm not sure I can forgive him for this." He studied her for a moment.

"I have much to forgive, myself. You are not alone with that struggle either. Some people can break your heart, but we still love them as

Gott loves us." Daniel felt that familiar warmth in his veins he got every time he thought about his father. If he hadn't taken them all away from the community, forced them to live in such a dark and dangerous world, *Mudder* and Michael might still be alive. Hannah wasn't the only one who needed to practice forgiveness.

She got to her feet. "Good night, Daniel." She was gone before he could find a reason to stop her.

Hannah lay on the bed, as Rosemary and M.J. cuddled beside her. She touched her cheek where moments ago Daniel had brushed away her tears. If only he could fix everything. She had no place in this world. But what really awaited her upon returning to Indiana? Magnolia Reynolds could not just return to her real estate job or her life before. Her house was likely already being foreclosed upon, her things no longer her own. What did she have to return to? That was the big question.

When the sound of thunder roared to the west, Hannah shuddered. Was she always going to be this afraid, waiting for something bad to happen, as Daniel had said? *It's just thunder.* She snuffed out the bedside lantern, drew up the quilt, placed an arm over Rosemary next to her. The last thing Hannah recalled was a pair of hazel eyes, warm calloused fingers, and the scent of rain and earth on a man who made her wish her life had started out very different than the hand dealt her.

Chapter Eleven

"The tracks go all the way around the lot." Vernon pointed at tire treads in the sloppy mud of the mill lot. Daniel followed the tire trail one way, meaning whoever had pulled in here left as soon as the rain started. The shower had started after ten o'clock, but only lasted less than an hour.

"I don't see anything missing. It wasn't thieves," Vernon added, a pinched look on his suntanned face.

"No, it wasn't thieves," Daniel said. He glanced past the lumberyard to the small incline. He walked the path day after day, knew it by heart. A man, a monster, could hide behind the cover of mounded earth and see his property easy enough. With binoculars, he could see everything.

"Probably some kids from town horsing around," Eli added.

"Well, nothing is missing, so how about we get that saw moving?" Daniel urged his men, keeping his true thoughts concealed. "I just need to check the answering machine and make a few calls this morning, and then I'll be out." Daniel had a phone call to make, that was for sure. Marshal Bates needed to know what he'd found, and Daniel needed to spend more time at home. He would change up his nightly routine too. Just in case this wasn't the first time someone had watched them.

The mysterious tire marks worried him all day. *Jah*, there were a dozen reasons for them, but there was one that was in the forefront of Daniel's thoughts as he walked home. Bates already had two men searching the area for clues, and even suggested leaving an officer to watch over the house. But that would draw attention, stirring up questions neither he nor Hannah were prepared to answer in their tight-knit community. But Daniel soon came to the realization that he couldn't refuse, not with his family's lives in danger. "*Gott*, watch over Hannah and the girls. Please hold them tight to You and give me whatever tools I need to protect them."

He stepped into the house; the strong aromas of cinnamon and cloves hung heavy in the air. Laughter spilled throughout the rooms. He tried to ignore the merriment, but found himself too weak to resist. Even after loss, there was laughter in his home. Was this not how things should be? His *onkel* spoke often on it. When a life was no more, we were to see that life as completed. It was hard to imagine his *mudder*—who should have had many years of life ahead of her, lots of grandchildren to coddle—a completed life. His father's decisions had taken that from her, had he not? And Michael. He too had made decisions that impacted others. How did *Gott* expect him just to look past those bad choices when they had followed him here, affected those he cared for? How was he supposed to simply forgive?

Removing his straw hat, he stepped farther into the house full of females. "Looks like you all are having too much fun in here," he said. Four beaming smiles greeted him. Even Catherine, who rarely smiled genuinely, did. M.J. ran to him and Daniel lifted her into his arms. He put on a happy face, for their sakes, but knowing that someone could, at any minute, take one of them from him, had his gut churning.

"Millie and *Mudder* are making pies and applesauce from all the apples. I got to smash the dough," M.J. said, slamming a tiny fist into her palm.

"Your Hannah here is going to teach me how

to make fried apple pies like her grandmother," Millie added. Daniel lifted a corner of his lips, glad she was more settled today than she had been last night. He hated that he would have to tell her after supper about what he'd found today. But he had to tell her. Keeping his true identity from her was one thing, but keeping a possible threat nearby a secret was entirely something else.

"Rosemary's crust is the best. Millie said so," M.J. said comically.

Daniel glanced around the kitchen, but didn't see Rosemary. He placed M.J. back on her bare feet.

"Where is Rosemary?" Daniel asked Hannah. Her smile faded into a solemn expression.

"She's behind the house. I think she needed a minute to herself."

"I'll go check on her." He kept his voice calm but his breathing was rapid. Knowing someone had been lurking about the farm and mill meant they needed to be always vigilant.

When he rounded the house, Daniel's heart skipped a beat to see there was no sign of Rosemary. Scouring the yard, he quickly found her on the rise, near his two beehives. He let out an exasperated breath and slowly took his time approaching.

Rosemary wasn't afraid of horses, and since

she was standing not ten feet from his hives, it seemed she wasn't afraid of bees either. She was entranced, watching them. Could this be what she needed? Nature nurturing her soul? He had sensed it each time they took a long stroll, *adventures* M.J. called them. Rosemary was always more relaxed outdoors.

When Daniel drew close, she sensed him and startled. "I'm sorry." She had been crying, alone, here on the hillside. It cut him, seeing this beautiful child heartbroken. She turned, ignoring him but not running away either. Daniel seized the opportunity to connect with her. "I lost my father too." Still, she stood stiffly, watching the bees jump from withering wildflower to milkweed. "I lost my home once also. I'm sorry you all had to leave so much behind."

Rosemary looked down at her hands, a blade of Timothy grass rolling between two fingers. He wanted to scoop her up, hold her and surround her with walls so strong, nothing dark could leak in. The surge of protectiveness grew stronger with her. She had witnessed a horrible thing, lost the one person meant to protect her and was a target. How could he even begin to help Rosemary when he couldn't fathom the battle being fought within her?

Rosemary turned shyly and slowly looked

up to him. Those big brown eyes, glistening, were Michael's eyes staring back at him. "How can Mommy laugh?" she murmured, then burst into another run of tears.

A bullet couldn't have this much power, he reckoned. Daniel's chest exploded, sending a huff of air out of his lungs. *She spoke.* He tried to rein in his emotions, but succumbed to them. He wrapped both his arms around her, and surprisingly, Rosemary buried herself deeper in his embrace.

He hadn't really cried since the day he'd buried his parents, but Rosemary's pain, her shattered little heart, broke him. He lifted her up and felt his heart jolt when her arms clung to his neck.

"I know, my *lieb*, I know," he crooned as he felt her arms squeeze tighter.

They remained there, holding one another in quiet tears. When he sat her back down on her feet, they both sat in the tall grass, watching the bees dance. "One day you will laugh again too."

"Does she not care?" To hear her tiny voice, so strong and yet so fragile, awoke something in him he never knew he possessed.

"It doesn't mean she doesn't care. She has been through a lot too, and worries for you and your sisters. It's good your *mudder* is able to laugh. She needed to feel good and Millie helped her. Don't hold it against her. *Gott* is working on all of you, trying to help you heal." Rosemary nodded. She understood more than a six-year-old girl should.

"How about I tell you about those hives? I could teach you about bees. I have books too." She wiped her face with her sleeve and looked up at him with curiosity in her eyes. He smiled tenderly at her. His heart was big enough for all of them. He loved her and felt she loved him too. "Maybe come spring, you can have her bring you back to the farm and we can harvest the honey together." He could only hope Hannah would, because he was too deep in love to never see them again.

Rosemary nodded. They reached a milestone today, and did it together.

Yes, today was a good day.

Hannah stepped out onto the porch as late October presented a spectacular view. Tall evergreens held fast to their bold emerald, while rustic gold, orange and reds competed wildly with a stunning sunset. It was breathtaking.

Everything about Daniel's world held the very essence of peace and an unchained freedom despite doing everything without conveniences. She laughed. It was funny, considering being Amish meant strict rules and yet freedom carried on the cool autumn breezes, through the shedding trees and over the lush lawn where her daughters ran barefoot and pushed one another on the rope swing Daniel had surprised them with that very first day. It was a balm of awakening, this moment right here. In all her life, she had never felt such calm, so near to God, whom she prayed to vigorously yet it seemed He seldom heard her.

She glanced down at her simple cornflower-blue dress, her white apron front, and realized the decision to come here was the best thing that had ever happened to her. She looked nothing like Magnolia Reynolds anymore, felt nothing like her either, and that meant everything.

Millie and Edith weren't like the women she knew back in Indiana. She had never had too many close friends, moving around far too much to make lasting connections. Yet, Hannah knew when she left this place, she would miss them both terribly.

She suspected Millie knew some, if not all, of her plight, but she also sensed Millie was not the kind of woman who would dig for details. Millie was also a widow who understood about bouts of loneliness, and though her late husband, Ben, had been an upstanding father and husband, they were both raising daughters alone. They shared a connection.

Whatever had transpired between Daniel and Rosemary yesterday, she was glad to see Rosemary more relaxed and excited at the prospect of learning about bees. Hannah would never tell a soul, but she had cried softly in her pillow that night when Daniel told her of his intentions to teach her daughter how to care for bees. It was a simple thing, and yet, it was so very much. He was the kind of man they deserved, rather than the father given to them and then stolen away. Would God find her terrible for such thoughts? She chided herself for such thinking. She knew Micah loved them, even if he never wanted children.

Stepping back inside to check on dinner, she pulled out the large roast from the oven and checked the meat for doneness. Spooning out most of the juices in a separate pan, Hannah added a healthy spoonful of flour, and began whisking the mixture over the back burner. She liked a thick gravy, and hoped Daniel did too. He never complained about her cooking. He never left the table without offering a thank-you either. She found herself looking forward to their chats on the porch, watching the day fade away as he updated her on what news the marshals had or how many saw blades he had gone through filling his latest lumber orders. All the while her daughters would be giggling inside, playing new games and finding joy without cable TV to appease them. How different their lives could have been if she weren't so anxious to please, so quick to fall in love. And if she were being honest, too gullible to know what was going on right underneath her nose for years.

Maybe she still was gullible, because it was growing more and more difficult to deny what those long looks Daniel sometimes tossed her way did to her.

Around three that afternoon, Daniel took a quick buggy ride into town to meet with the local sheriff and pick up a few things Hannah had scribbled down for him at the store. He was glad the sheriff was taking the threat seriously and agreed to keep Hannah and the children's identities secret. At least there would be others looking out for them. Eli and Vernon could handle things well enough at the mill. Daniel needed to be closer to home until this was over. And if the marshal's gut instincts were right, it would all be over soon. Daniel wasn't sure how he felt about that.

Now instead of working, he was buying protective bee gear for a little girl so she had something to look forward to. He should be home, watching over the farm, making arrangements for the mill, not shopping. Then the thought hit him. It was time Hannah learned how to handle a horse and buggy.

Thirty minutes later, he entered the house with two paper bags in his arms. He had every intention of informing Hannah that she would be doing her own shopping from now on. When he reached the kitchen doorway, he paused and his earlier frustrations vanished. She looked so pretty in her new blue dress, her cheeks flushed from canning what looked to be apples, and that one curly tendril escaped and clinging to her delicate neck. She was humming too, a clear indication she was in a good mood.

"New dress?" he asked. Hannah startled, bringing one hand to her chest.

"You're home early," she exclaimed, as she turned back to the stove. "And yes, Edith is spoiling me. I think I want to learn to sew them myself. It isn't right she has to go to all this trouble. I am sure I can get the hang of it."

Daniel didn't doubt that one bit. "I'm sure she will be more than happy to teach you." A hint of something resembling hope rushed through him. Hannah, learning more about their life, and his life. Would she ever consider staying? It was a fanciful thought, one he knew better than to entertain. He was Amish, and she was *Englisch*. She was Michael's wife and he was simply the man who promised to look after her.

And what could he possibly offer her? Daniel had seen it for himself, the fancy clothes and expensive cars. Michael had taken her from being an orphan to living in a big house with everything her heart desired. Daniel could never give her more than this old house and a sawmiller's promise. He never could measure up to his brother, and after seeing his beautiful wife and falling for those sweet children, he knew he never would. They deserved everything this world had to offer them.

He reached up to touch the scar on his neck, now hidden under new growth. Here he was playing a part for his brother again, only this time a real heart was at stake.

"I think it's time you learn to drive a buggy," he announced.

"But… I can't do that," Hannah said a bit too quickly. Daniel dropped both grocery bags on the table and fished out the bee gear he had purchased for Rosemary.

"You can. I think shopping is better suited for you than me," Daniel added in a sharp tone.

"Because I'm a woman?" Her chin lifted.

"You're better at it than I am." He smirked. "City girls are experts, if memory serves me well."

"Not all city girls. I hate shopping and I know nothing about horses. Don't presume you know me, Daniel Raber. Besides, Edith says I can hire a driver if I really need to go anywhere." Even angry she was adorable. Daniel tried ignoring how much so.

"Drivers cost money."

"And what of the dangers? You can't expect me to go shopping with a maniac out there. And I have my own money, so don't bother using that as an excuse."

"Marshal Bates has men all over this town. They would be staked out in the front yard if they wouldn't draw so much attention. The sheriff plans on driving by the house a few times a day and checking to see if any new faces have come into town. If it was indeed Corsetti, they will find him."

"How can you be so sure?" Was she going to quarrel about trusting him, a stranger, again?

"I put my trust in *Gott*," he said, looking at her intensely.

"That's a foolish thing to do," Hannah murmured.

"I would love to argue this more with you, wife," he said, "but I have a date with a bee charmer this evening. Tomorrow, Edith will watch the children while I teach you how to handle a horse and buggy. Maybe you will learn a thing or two about trust then."

Daniel grinned and strolled out the door, leaving Hannah speechless.

Chapter Twelve

Hannah clasped the buggy reins in both hands and tried not to tremble. Her heart sped up, but she really wanted to do this. Not for Daniel, of course, but for herself. There was something satisfying in knowing how to handle oneself no matter what the circumstances. Fear always drove her, but Hannah learned long ago to power through those feelings.

"Now just pull back slowly if you feel she is getting ahead of you," Daniel coached from the seat next to her. November was almost upon them. A crisp breeze threatened, but she was sweating bullets thanks to her jangled nerves. Despite her fear of a half-ton animal, Hannah did what she always did: she continued on. She gave Maybelle a light tap of the reins and clicked her tongue as Daniel instructed. The horse moved gingerly, no jerk or eagerness in her aged flesh. That put her more at ease. She couldn't imagine handling Colt alone. The gelding was strong, eager and always ready to go. Maybelle was older and wiser, and Hannah sensed she knew exactly who the driver was.

"Veer right here. We should stick to the back roads."

Hannah did as he asked. "But this is pavement. Back roads aren't usually paved."

"It's on the way," Daniel said with a hint of humor in his tone. He was having way too much fun seeing her uncomfortable. "I told you there was nothing to it."

Hannah chuckled. "I bet if I let go of the reins, she would bring us back to the house easy enough."

"*Jah*, she would. Would you have preferred I hitched Colt up for you?" He lifted a brow.

"I think Maybelle will work fine for me for now." She could practice more, learn to harness the mare all by herself. Then she could do her own shopping and not depend on Edith and Daniel so much. He was right, but she didn't have to tell him that. Maybe if she got good enough, Hannah could take the girls and visit Edith. They hadn't seen inside her home yet, only the outside when they dropped the children off earlier. And Millie. Hannah had been yearning to see the orchard Millie spoke so much about. She had grown very close to both women and looked forward to spending more time cultivating those friendships as much as she could.

As tempting as it was to imagine her life here, Hannah knew she was no Margaret Sayer. She was the outsider. She wasn't born into communities full of unwavering faith. She was born into a world where nothing lasted and only the strong survived. Believing in God, praying for miracles, was one thing. Submitting wasn't even hard to fathom, but to become part of something, this lifestyle of faith and community, was a mirage. Nothing good ever lasted, she knew that all too well.

Besides, it wasn't like Daniel saw her as anything more than the mother of the three girls he had come to adore and protect. It was her children he cared for, and for that she was grateful.

A few minutes later, Hannah veered the buggy onto the gravel road Daniel pointed out. She had been right about backroads and felt her muscles tense as the buggy bounced over uneven ground. "So where does this trust part come in?"

"The horse must trust you and you must trust him, or else accidents happen," he said.

"So that's where I went wrong in life," she

quipped. "I never had a horse." His laugh filled the evening air.

"But you have three wonderful girls."

"Three amazing, beautiful and perfect little girls," she corrected, meeting his smile with one of her own. Daniel was easygoing and seemed to already forget their previous quarrel. Micah would have never forgotten so easily.

"Do you ever feel guilty? For lying to all of your friends and family?"

"We have only withheld the truth to keep you—and them—safe, but *jah*, I do."

They rode in silence, up one road, down another. Hannah tried to focus on the evening, the scenery and Maybelle, but all she could focus on was the man next to her and how she disrupted his life.

An hour later, and one panicky instant with a speeding car, Daniel leaned back in the buggy seat and pretended to enjoy the ride back toward his *onkel*'s. Joshua had told Hannah the sign at the end of his and Edith's lane that read Poverty's Knob was there from the previous owners, and considering how empty his pockets stayed, he couldn't bear taking it down. Hannah had laughed about it before they left the girls to bake and play with Edith, but she wasn't laughing now as she sat stiffly beside him and in total control of the reins. Hannah, as he was beginning to see, learned at a masterful pace, but he sensed she didn't like control, or the responsibility that came with it. She didn't like lying either, which had earned her his utmost respect.

"So will I be driving Catherine to school in the morning?"

Hannah shot him a quick look. "I've spoken to her and she's finally agreed to go. I still think it isn't safe. What if those tire tracks were from someone spying on us?"

"No way of knowing for sure, but there are many looking into who made those tracks. School will be good for her and she will be surrounded by others all day." Hannah nodded her head. She understood his logic, but Daniel knew fear still rested in her mind.

"I like driving the buggy on the pavement better," she commented. He listened to the clip-clop of Maybelle's hooves striking in cadence. "The gravel is loose, and it feels like we may slide. I'm glad she handles so well." He watched her fingers tighten on the reins. She was letting the new sensation of control warm her. It made a lot of sense. So much of her life was out of her control, grabbing a piece of it wherever she could helped her gain something resembling strength. For it was strength he saw when he looked at her.

"Tell me more about the girls. How they were before you came here." She shot him a curious look, then focused back on the old gravel road ahead that he'd insisted on. It was easy for him to forget sometimes what connected them. Thankfully, she didn't press his motives and assumed he was simply making idle conversation.

"Well, after three false alarms, Catherine was born nineteen days late. Oh, and her first word was *no*," Hannah laughed.

"I suspected as much," Daniel said on a chuckle.

The cool breeze, mingled with the slow pace of Maybelle, had Hannah shivering and he quickly shucked his coat, wrapping it around her. *"Danki,"* she said, slipping her arms into the long sleeves. He knew Hannah was a small woman, but in his coat, she looked even smaller.

"Catherine was always independent and strong, even as a *boppli*." Daniel lifted a brow at her use of the Amish word for *baby*. Since her arrival, she had been reluctant to use his language. "She walked when she wanted, spoke full sentences when she was ready and even ate when she chose no matter the hour.

Catherine lives life in her own timing, you could say. But—" she glanced his way "—whatever life throws at her, she will do well."

"And Martha Jane? What of her?"

"Besides *Mama*, her first words were *go-go*." Hannah broke into a warm smile. "And she was born early, of course."

Daniel laughed. "Of course, she had much to see in this world." Hannah chuckled with him. Did she know her eyes twinkled when she forgot why she was here?

"Exactly. She has always been on the go and never met a stranger she didn't want to be friends with."

"Or a rooster," Daniel added. It was nice, sharing this together. He wondered what she was like before too. Hannah had given him glimpses into her past, but nothing substantial. Talking about her children was a good distraction as she handled the horse and buggy. Her white-knuckle grip had already loosened again.

"Believe it or not, Rosemary was quite the adventurer. You should have seen her, Daniel." Her breath hitched and he nearly regretted broaching the topic. "She walked at seven months. When she was three, she rode her bike without training wheels. She used to chase bugs and catch bees with her fingers. She used to pick flowers." When she turned to face him again, the tears were falling down her cheeks, her grip of the reins going slack. "She used to sing all the time. She had the sweetest voice. And she had imaginary friends." The more she grieved for her daughter's lost innocence, the more her hands shook. Daniel took the reins from her and guided Maybelle into a hayfield to their right. He didn't dare tell her that Rosemary had spoken to him. Not now. Hannah had tried coaxing words out of her since they arrived and he could see how it broke her heart when nothing worked.

When she covered her face with her hands, Daniel pulled her to him, enveloping her with arms that would help carry this burden for her. "It will get better. It already has. Surely, you see that.

"*Gott* promises us that suffering doesn't last. We must see each new day for the blessing it truly is. Live in it with intent." The scent of her hair, the weight of her head against his chest felt right, and Daniel wanted to keep her there in his stronghold. "I'm sorry your husband is not here with you, helping you through this." Did she still mourn Michael? Did she wish he were here instead of him?

She looked up at him. "I failed him so badly. I tried so hard to make him happy but I failed.

And the girls, they wanted to spend more time with him but there was always a case, a person in need, something more important than his own family. Is it wrong that I'm angry at him when it's me who failed him?" She sobbed harder. "I made his life miserable. I ruined everything."

"That can't be true, Hannah. He failed to follow the law, that's all. I'm sure he loved you and the girls more than you know. Some people just can't show love the same way as others do. None of this is your fault."

"Daniel, I couldn't convince him to go to church. I couldn't find a way to show him how important he was to his children. He wasn't happy. He didn't want us. What's worse, he died unhappy."

"*Nee*, I don't think that's true. You're just upset. Your husband had you, and three wonderful children." Daniel pulled away from her. How could she think herself not enough for any man? How could his brother not see the pearl he had been given?

"He left this world with no faith, no love and no idea how badly those little girls loved him. Because he didn't love me anymore, they suffered. Because I wasn't enough for him, my children thought their father didn't even like them. What kind of woman is given the perfect life and messes it up this badly?"

In her sudden breakdown, Hannah had told him everything he needed, but wished he didn't know. Daniel's jaw tightened. Michael had become no different than their father. He'd never been satisfied. Their own mother cried tears of guilty burdens, just like he imagined Hannah had. She'd tried to help *Daed* keep his faith, follow the straight and narrow. Instead, he abandoned everything they knew to be right, for *Englisch* things. His heart cracked anew. Michael too was a lost soul, and the pain etched in Hannah's eyes confirmed it.

"We are only responsible for our own actions. You can't blame yourself for another's sins." He squeezed her hand.

"He took all of it for granted. He stole and lied and put his children in danger. He was so kind, in the beginning. But you're right." She straightened and wiped her face. "He took it all for granted, didn't he?" Daniel nodded, sensing she needed his assurances, though learning about Michael this way hurt something awful. "Bryan said he had been stealing from these mob people for a long time. Why do people do that? Why does love just stop?" She thought he had the answers, desperately wanted him to have them. If she knew the truth, it might give her some closure, but Daniel couldn't tell her about Michael, what had shaped him into the man he became, no matter how much he wanted to right now.

"I don't know." Though part of him did. Putting oneself before others always invited sin.

"He wasn't the kind of person you would have liked. I was married to a man I didn't even know." She laughed. "Talk about repeating your mistakes."

Daniel didn't laugh. Hannah was the smartest person he knew. He didn't believe she made many mistakes and didn't want to be considered one. He couldn't stand seeing her like this. "I'm sorry he hurt you, but I feel he loved you, just maybe not the way he should have." Michael had chosen his lot in life, just as his *daed* had, but he would have never married Hannah if he hadn't loved her. That much he was sure of. How long would Daniel carry around this hardness in his heart for them? Their mistakes weren't his to carry. Was that not what he had just tried to convince Hannah of?

It was time to put the past aside, stop dwelling in the shadows as Hannah was clearly doing herself. They needed to forgive. Forgive those who took advantage, who didn't care enough, who took the wrong paths. There was no way either of them could move forward without it.

Hannah had already endured abandonment from early on, and when she looked up at him, he saw the pain of it again in her teary blue eyes. Daniel felt his heart thunder, felt the ache of holding back when all he wanted to do was surround her in a love so great doubt had no place there.

It was time to separate the past from the present. "I know this isn't easy on you, handling all this alone, but…"

"But I am not alone, am I?" she said sharply, and he sensed his world was shifting again.

"*Nee.* We are never alone, Hannah. *Gott* is always there. He will wipe away your tears."

"I know that. I think I've always known that." She sniffed back another run of tears. "And so are you, Daniel Raber," she said. "You don't see it. What a treasure a few minutes of your attention does for them. My children feel safe with you. They trust you. I think they love you."

"They are easy to love," Daniel admitted out loud and felt there was more that needed to be said, but didn't dare cross that line.

"Why haven't you ever married?" she asked him. "You would make a wonderful father."

Because I was waiting for the right one, he wanted to say.

Instead, he teased her. "I am married, am I not?" He shrugged. "I never took the time for it. I dated a bit when I was younger."

"Did you have a girlfriend when you lived in Chicago?" Daniel was surprised by the question and felt his cheeks grow warm. "You probably dated dozens of girls. I bet Margaret isn't the only one in Miller's Creek who delivered a dish or two at your door."

"Do you really want to know this stuff?" he asked her. Hannah wiped the remaining tears from her face and nodded. "Okay. I dated a couple women, but none really suited me. They were more interested in material things than I was. Their faith wasn't sound and that meant the most to me. One cannot build a home on a weak foundation." He looked out over the field as the light chased shadows. "Not many in your world can accept mine. I never made it a secret that I had hopes of returning to my Amish roots. I was always honest about that."

"I could imagine how that went over," Hannah laughed. "I can't lie, when they told me I was coming here, what was expected of us, if I hadn't been so numb from all that had just happened, I would have probably run too."

"But you didn't." He stared at her intently,

searching for what his heart was aching for but feared being denied.

"No, I didn't," she said softly. With that, his heart stirred.

"And now?" A flicker of surprise raced over her features. Did she like being an Amish bride? Would leaving be something she would regret? His heart yearned to know the answers.

"I think what you and Edith and Millie have is something special. I have never known community like you have. Millie and Edith are... friends. Not the kind you work with or who happen to be married to your spouse's friends, but real friends."

"So I'm not your friend." He tried looking offended.

"*Nee*, you're my husband, remember," she teased. "I've never canned applesauce before or made homemade cheese, but I like it." She sounded like M.J. and Daniel couldn't smother his reaction. "Don't laugh."

"I'm not laughing at you. I'm glad to hear we have made such an impression." In this light, the shimmering in her eyes pulled him in.

"You have, Daniel," she said in a softer, more serious tone. "Made an impression, I mean. My children feel loved here. That is a special thing, even if it's short-lived."

"It is." He shifted, angling his body to face

her. For a brief moment, he forgot she was Michael's. Forgot the promise he had made that first morning. He wanted to show her just how much she deserved. "We all need and deserve love And love isn't short-lived or temporary, Hannah. Real love, it's everlasting." He never planned to have these feeling for…his wife, and now he wanted more. The urge to kiss her, draw her closer, had never been harder to resist. All he had to do was lean down. If he were just given the chance. Not as Michael's brother or the stranger that took her in, but the man he knew himself to be.

"The kind of love that never stops," Hannah whispered, her cool blue eyes looking up under long lashes still damp from crying. He lifted a hand and slowly cradled her cheek. The cool of her flesh collided with the warmth of his hand and he felt her give slowly.

A truck honked as it drove by, a customer whom Daniel recognized driving it, jolting them both back to the present. "I'm sorry," he quickly apologized, withdrawing his hand. "We should get back." How could he have almost kissed her?

Chapter Thirteen

Hannah was beside herself. Catherine hated school and there was no reassuring her. Being shifted from home to home, Hannah remembered what it was like starting a new school, how cruel some kids could be. And just four days in, Catherine had become the center of Jesse Plank and his teasing friends' world. No one liked being called names, or picked on. After supper, Hannah slipped outside to join Daniel for their regular nightly talk. The man seemed to have an answer for everything. Had he gone through some of the same things when he lived outside of the Amish community?

"It's getting colder." Hannah shivered as November winds blew over them. "I should probably learn to knit or something. The girls will need scarves." The swing Daniel and Joshua had hung in the oak tree swayed in the breeze.

"I should start hauling over more wood. Winter will be here before we know it," Daniel added, leaning on his post while Hannah leaned on hers. This had become their habit, a routine that they each looked forward to but never spoke about.

She stared out over the scenery. The land was slowly losing its autumn plumage, preparing itself for its winter slumber. She tried to imagine what it would look like covered in snow. Would the girls get to go sleighing on the neighboring hillsides and make snowmen? She shoved back the thought, and tried to focus on the reality. This was Daniel's home, not hers, and if things were on track as Daniel thought, then soon all of this would be over. No sense getting more comfortable than they already were. But he'd almost kissed her. Could she have simply imagined that too?

"I'd like to take Catherine to work with me tomorrow," Daniel said, bringing her back to the present. He cared for her children. Children were easy to love, he had said. Like puppies, all cute and sweet and clumsily adorable. At least her girls had this love now, when they needed it most. She thanked God each night for that. Though she hoped He would provide answers, the right words for her, when the time came to depart.

"Why?"

"Eli needs to know this teasing his *sohn* is tossing out has consequences. I won't have Catherine treated unkindly." Daniel's frown indicated he too was angry Catherine was having a hard time fitting in.

"You could just talk to Eli. I'm sure if he knows Jesse is calling her names, he will see it stops." Or Hannah could talk with Jesse's mother, Sara, herself. No mother would stand by her child being cruel to others.

"I could, but this way is better." Daniel shifted, his back now resting on the post. He looked as handsome as that first morning in his pale green shirt and suspenders and carrying a breakfast tray. "We cannot always stop others from acting a certain way, but we can decide how we handle it."

"And by handling it, you mean skipping school instead of turning the other cheek?" Her words earned her a narrowed look.

"Catherine has been through plenty and even little girls need a break." Hannah warmed to his absolute observations of her children. He continued, "I can let her answer the phone in the office. Maybe take her to lunch in town, just the two of us."

"Just the two of you?" Hannah asked, slightly befuddled.

"*Jah,* a day with my pretend daughter," he said, sliding his thumbs into his suspenders. "I hear it's a thing." He shrugged.

Hannah managed not to liquefy into a pool of mush right there. "I think that would be lovely," she choked out. Her daughter would have one of those luncheons she always dreamed of, the kind where you were made the center of your father's world. Did he know what he was promising? "That's very sweet of you, Daniel."

"I can be sweet," he teased, puffing out his chest playfully.

"And humble, I see," she mocked. If only all men were measured by this one, then marriages would be happy-ever-after and all children would feel they mattered. She suspected when Daniel Raber loved, it was a gift worth cherishing.

They grew silent. Above them, stars blinked to life. "So many stars," she muttered, in awe with the display above her. One of the few fond memories she still held dear was Anna telling her stories under the stars. She hadn't done that with the girls before. She would, before the air grew much colder. They were supposed to go camping that very weekend their world unraveled.

There were so many things Hannah had

been denied in her childhood, but her daughters deserved all the wonderful moments and lessons of simplicity that might mold them into better people. And Daniel. They deserved being cared for by a man like Daniel Raber. She didn't need to hear the words to know he loved her children. It showed in the gleam in his eyes, the laughter in his voice, and in the way he attentively treated each of them.

Daniel sat on the top step, legs outstretched, and leaning back on his elbows. He was in no rush to end the evening and neither was she. Patting the wooden plank beside him, he urged for her to sit too.

Hannah lowered down beside him. He smelled of sawdust and sweat. Was she falling under the same infatuation as her daughters? Pondering what she was falling into, Hannah settled back and faced the glittering of night.

"He counts the number of the stars and calls them by their name," Daniel said.

She glanced over and noted he was still looking up. "That's a psalm," she said. "Though don't ask me which one," Hannah half laughed. Daniel looked over, and rested his hazel eyes on her. As long as she lived, Hannah would never find eyes so honest, so engaging.

"I'm not sure which one it is either." Daniel's lips quirked into a grin.

Hannah rubbed her arms up and down, took in a deep breath of cold night air. "I have never breathed so easily."

"It's slower, harder, a more restricted life here, but yes—" he pulled his gaze from her and looked out again "—it's easy to breathe in."

"The pace gives you time to think, enjoy your hard work, and having no phone helps." She thought she would have missed having her cell phone by now. Oddly, Hannah hadn't missed it at all. Who else did she need to talk to? Everyone she knew or cared about was right here.

"You miss it? Living in Indiana, living the *Englisch* life?" He studied her again.

"I miss what could have been, but no, I don't think I do. I like having time to do things right. Not being rushed. I missed spending time with the girls when Micah insisted I went back to work. How about you? Do you miss Chicago?"

"I missed being here when I was in Chicago. *Nee*, I'm right where I am meant to be." His heart had been set long ago and she could see that in his reply.

"I've never been confident like that. God sort of tossed me around and I made the best of wherever I landed."

"*Gott* always has a plan, even if we don't see it."

"Yes, He does. I'm learning that better now. Edith speaks so much of me being here for a reason. Like it was meant to happen," she half laughed. "It has helped the girls deal with everything. They are adjusting well. We have enjoyed our time here with you, Daniel. I want you to know that. It means a lot to all of us."

"I like having you all here too," he said in that deep voice that often made her shudder. "I made you a promise. To offer you shelter and safety, until it's safe for you all to leave, but I will miss you all terribly."

Hannah took a shaky breath. Her daughters were easy to love, but a part of her wanted to know how he felt about her. Would he miss her? "I've been meaning to tell you, the beard looks good on you. Edith told me why you are growing it."

His cheeks glowed pink. "*Jah*, it's one of the rules of the Order. Married men don't shave."

"And you are a married man now," she said, grinning.

"You still haven't brought me lunch yet," he said, leaning closer to her.

"You still want me to bring you lunch?" His voice had her floating, her breath quickening.

"Catherine did tell Millie and Margaret that

you do bring lunch to see me some days." He lifted a brow, taking one corner of his smile with it.

"But that was just…"

He chuckled deep, and low, and very unsettling. "A lie. So, let's fix that."

"I still don't think it's a good idea, Daniel."

"You did run off my only prospect for a girlfriend, did you not?" he teased. She wasn't so off-kilter. Hannah had forgotten how men and women interacted, and it was clear Daniel was flirting.

"I guess I did." She smiled cunningly. "I'm sure the girls would like that very much."

"And you? Would you like that?" Was he just curious, or did he really want to know? Did she dare let her heart fall for another man, knowing he too would one day grow tired of her?

Looking at him, she moved her fingers toward the scar slowly being camouflaged in his newly grown facial hair. "Where did this come from?" She didn't touch him, but felt the warmth of him being so close.

"My *bruder*," he said flatly, and she withdrew her hand immediately. Hannah watched him tense. Daniel had refused to talk about Michael before. Keeping silent, she waited. She wouldn't push. After a time, Daniel began to relax. Leaning forward, elbows on knees, she could see him battling with sharing this part of himself.

"I looked up to him, when I was young. He was just a year older than me." He threaded his fingers together, before continuing. "When we were *kinner*, he was always doing stupid things. Getting stuck in trees, painting the old deacon's dog and other things I would rather not say." His voice grew more gravelly but she could tell he had enjoyed that time in his life. She'd never had siblings of her own. Daniel had lost his parents but she was beginning to realize that he had lost his brother too. That had to be why it was so hard to speak of him. A year apart, they were most likely very close.

"Painting a dog?" Micah had once painted a dog, he had told her. Something about a grumpy old man telling his parents he caught him smoking cigarettes with friends.

"*Jah*," Daniel chuckled. "*Mudder* was madder than a wet cat over that one." Hannah could imagine.

"As a boy I thought he was the bravest person in the world. He was fearless. Nothing scared him. I got to tag along on what is it M.J. calls them, 'ventures?" They both laughed. "Michael was a lot like our *daed*. He never wanted this life and when *Daed* moved us to the city, things just changed. When he was around eleven or so, he wanted to be Indiana Jones, got a toy whip and that hat, you know the one, for his birthday." Hannah nodded but remained quiet as he worked through this telling of his brother.

Daniel pointed to the scar on his neck. "This was from him practicing knocking a can off my shoulder." Daniel cocked his head. "Michael had a way of leaving scars behind him."

When his knowing eyes held her, recognition slowly registered and Hannah bristled. *Indiana Jones. Painting dogs.* Could it be possible? That grin... She would have never guessed it. The story wasn't just Daniel's, it was Micah's too. What a fool she was not to have seen it sooner. Even the way his lips tightened when holding back, just like Rosemary's did. She shivered, but not from the cold. Was this really happening? She staggered to her feet.

"Are you okay?" Daniel reached to steady her but she jerked away from him quickly.

"Oh…yes. I'm sorry. I should go check on the girls. Good night, Daniel." Hannah rushed into the house feeling more betrayed than ever. She had fallen for another man who was a liar too.

Chapter Fourteen

Daniel did as he said he would and dragged an angry nine-year-old to the mill with him. Catherine looked no happier to be at work with him than going to school and dealing with Jesse Plank. That frown was in danger of becoming a permanent stain on her little face. When the teenaged years arrived, Hannah would be in trouble.

"I'm only nine," Catherine sassed, crossing both slender arms over her chest. "Isn't making me work like against the law or something?" Daniel rubbed a tense nerve at the back of his neck, and forced a smile. He could either pull his hair out or laugh dealing with Hannah's eldest. Then he remembered that little pocket of information he'd kept stashed away for just the right moment.

"Well, I'll tell you the truth. I brought you

because I could really use your help. Are you any *gut* with numbers?" He knew she was. Hannah had mentioned how advanced Catherine was in math in her former school.

Her blue eyes, just like Hannah's, lit up, but she refused to answer him. Daniel continued. "And it so happens that Jesse Plank's dad works here. He talks all the time about how Jesse can muck twenty stalls in one afternoon."

"I can muck a stall. You made me, remember." She started tapping her foot against the wooden floor.

"*Jah*, and you do good work. Sometimes Eli brings Jesse here to work when school is out. That boy can count lumber footages faster than I can." He tested and she still remained stubbornly poised. "I guess boys just have better heads for such things. I thought maybe having an apprentice, someone to learn how to do the books and so forth, would be good for business. It was just a silly idea. I can run you back to school if you'd rather. I should have known this wasn't something you could do." Daniel opened the office door and waited for her to follow. After two long minutes, it worked like a charm. Challenging her, and using Jesse Plank to do it, was all the kindling he needed to strike that fire.

"No boy is smarter than me, especially Jesse

Plank." She pulled off her jacket and tossed it over his office chair. "What does an apprentice do?"

Daniel had to do everything in his power not to smile.

By noon, Daniel stepped back into his mill office and found the floors swept, the windows scrubbed, two phone messages written surprisingly in neat handwriting on a notepad, and a stack of receipts and orders he had scattered about, organized. There was no way this child was only nine. Daniel was more than impressed. He was shocked by her hidden talents. Now if he could just knock down that last remaining wall."I promised you lunch, and you have certainly earned it." Daniel motioned for her to follow him.

"Where are we going?" she asked as she followed him to the buggy and climbed in.

Daniel climbed up beside her and felt the warmth of accomplishment seeing her eager smile. "It's a surprise."

Just as they neared the diner in town, the skies opened up and it started to pour. Daniel quickly parked the buggy, tethered Colt and pulled Catherine into his arms. "Come on, munchkin. Can't have you getting your pretty *kapp* soaked." He covered her head with his straw hat, though it did little to ward off the downpour, and ran for the diner door, her giggles floating behind them.

Daniel guided her toward the center of the diner to an empty booth. "Let's sit over here."

"Why are we here?" She slid in the booth, her hair damp under her *kapp*.

"What can I get you two?" the waitress asked as she offered a handful of napkins to Catherine. "You are soaked, sweetie. How about some warm soup? Maybe a hot chocolate?" Catherine looked to Daniel, for permission perhaps.

"Order whatever you want," he encouraged.

"I would really like a hot dog and the hot chocolate too, thank you very much." Daniel was impressed with her manners.

"Same for me, with french fries please." The diner was well known for their homemade fries and, of course, pie. They ate in silence, sharing the fries, as they watched people stroll by the large diner window.

Daniel noted the green car sitting out front. The same one he recalled pulling in the same time he was running with Catherine in his arms toward the diner. The man behind the wheel wore dark glasses but the tint of the windows revealed little else. Daniel didn't know everyone in town, but he was certain this person didn't live in the area. No one got in or out of the car, and Daniel held his attention on it—and the shadowy driver—until it slowly backed out into the road and drove away. He would be sure to report what he saw to Bates soon.

When he turned to Catherine again, she dipped a fry into her ketchup and gave him a curious peek. "You're not, like, an undercover cop, are you?"

"No," he chuckled. "Just a Plain man who makes his living in lumber."

She studied him closer, chewed her mouthful. "So you are a real Amish person, helping us just because Bryan made you?"

"He didn't make me, I volunteered." Daniel claimed a fry, dipped it in her ketchup and ate it.

"So you're helping us because you want to?" She handed him a fry, a silent truce perhaps.

"I care very much about what happens to all of you." Catherine stared at him for another moment, processing his words. It was true she didn't rush her thoughts unless angry. Daniel gave her all the time she needed to consider her next question, because he knew she had more questions. He just hoped he had the right answers.

Breaking the silence between them, the

waitress came over. "Can I get you two some dessert, maybe a coffee?" she asked.

"Ice cream and coffee would be nice, *danki*," Daniel replied. "Is that okay, *dochder*?" He smiled across the table. Catherine gave the waitress a nod but shot Daniel a narrowed look.

Then the waitress returned with their ice cream. "Here you go, you two. Rain looks to be letting up." She smiled at Catherine. "You might get home dryer than you were when you arrived." She patted Catherine's shoulder, gave Daniel a wry smile and walked away.

"Are you going to eat all of that?" he teased, reaching over with his spoon and stealing a bite of ice cream from her bowl.

"My dad was a detective," Catherine said, choosing her next bite carefully.

"He was very important, *jah*. You must miss him."

She shrugged. "He helped find people who got lost." She licked her spoon, stared out the window in a daze. "He was like a superhero."

"That he was," Daniel added.

"Real dads are busy. They work to pay for stuff and don't have time for ice cream and stuff." Her tone grew bitter. "You're not a real dad."

He let the insult roll off his sleeve. This was just a child trying to understand her place in the world. A child grieving for what she'd lost. "*Nee*, I am not. I like eating ice cream too well." Daniel snuck another bite from her bowl, half-teasing, but when she looked up to him again, he froze. She was serious. Had Michael never spent time with his children? Hannah had been angry when she said those things, but Daniel hadn't thought she meant Michael had never done *anything* with them. He thought Hannah only implied his busy life left him few moments to spare. A man's first duty was to his family. To teach his children they are valued, loved, and how to value and love others. He put the spoon down, and felt the first wave of nausea come about. Catherine's shoulders straightened; he could see that hard stubbornness making her all cold again.

"Catherine, I'm sorry about what has happened."

"It's not your fault," she muttered. "She doesn't think we know, but I do. I know he wasn't a good guy. I heard Bryan and the tall guy say it. They say he took money and lied a lot."

"I'm sorry you heard that."

"I'm not telling my sisters." She pushed her spoon around the melting ice cream as if lost in the swirls and textures.

Daniel reached across the table, took hold

of her tiny hand. "I know I'm not your *daed*. That this is all pretend until the man who hurt your father is found, but while we have this time together, I say, let's make the best of it."

"Like how?"

"We take the time to talk, maybe eat ice cream more often. If something bothers you, I want you to be able to talk to me, and your *mudder*. It bothers her when you're not happy and she doesn't know how to fix it." She pulled her hand free and toyed with her ice cream again.

"She always has to fix everything. When Dad wouldn't take Rosemary camping like he promised, she said she was going to take us. She always has to do what he forgets." She bit her bottom lip and looked up to him again. "I'll just talk to you so she doesn't have so much to worry about, since you're my pretend dad and all."

Progress, with a dash of guilt added. Would Hannah be upset at him for communicating with both Rosemary and Catherine? "She's your *mudder*. No one other than *Gott* will love you more than her."

"I know that." She took another bite of softened vanilla. "I'm nine, not stupid. She acts happy, but I know she's sad."

"My *mudder* did that. She was sad a lot, but we never knew."

"What was she sad about?" Catherine cocked her head and asked. They were connecting, bonding, and she was opening up to him. And Daniel found it wasn't that hard at all.

"My *daed*, well, he was a strange man."

"How?"

"Well, he thought living here, being Amish, was a terrible way to live."

"It's not so bad." She shrugged and took another spoonful of ice cream. Daniel grinned.

"He had strange thoughts, and tended to forget us sometimes too. He moved us away from the community to live among strangers." Kind of how he predicted Catherine felt right now. "My *mudder* helped us fit in, but *Daed* only cared about other things." Daniel had no intention of elaborating on the kinds of things that came first to his father.

"Our daddy did that too. He didn't like being home, or having kids," she said on a sigh. Her honesty cut him. "Especially M.J. He never talked to her." Was that why she craved friendships? Daniel shifted in the booth seat. "Sometimes he would look at Rosemary and make funny faces."

Because she looks like her grandmother, the

mother he left behind weeping, Daniel thought. Would he ever be able to make up for the pain his brother inflicted?

"We may never understand everyone, but *Gott* promises we are never alone. Even when family fails us, we have community. Community is important to the Amish. You always have others to care for you, look out for you, as *Gott* intended."

"I like the name Catherine, you know, but don't tell." She pinned him with a sharp look that Hannah often possessed.

"Catherine is a very strong name. It means pure. Catherines are understanding, and they take their time choosing their path. They do well at everything. They listen before speaking and are well loved within their family."

"I can do that." Her shoulders rose. "Listen and do well."

"I know you can. I could use some help at the mill on a regular basis." Her face lit up. "Don't get excited. We still must ask your *mudder*. You could help after school and maybe some Saturdays when I'm already working over there. Never without me."

"Really?"

"*Jah*. But you have to ignore Jesse Plank and finish all your chores. Plus, I expect you to help your *mudder*."

"I can help Mom, but can I hit Jesse Plank just once? Mom says girls don't hit, but boys shouldn't need to be hit."

Daniel chuckled. "Well, a good *maedel* would never do that." Then he leaned closer. "Even if it is well deserved. I have a feeling after today you won't have a problem with Jesse." Daniel had it on good authority Jesse was going to be punished for all his teasing.

"And after hot chocolate, he let me have two scoops of ice cream. I couldn't finish it and it melted but he never got mad," Catherine told Hannah as she tucked her into bed. She never thought she would see her child look happy again and it warmed her heart.

"Sounds like you had a really good day," Hannah said. Of course she did. Her own uncle loved her and spent the day with her. Hannah had been a fool, yet again, letting her heart be swept away by Daniel. She knew now Bryan bringing her here wasn't a coincidence. Daniel was Micah's brother. Another lie Micah had told her. He'd said his family was dead, that he was all alone in the world like her. That was how they had connected, why she'd kissed him that first time. It was the first lie of many and now Daniel too was a liar. Worse, Bryan had known it. She couldn't trust anyone.

"I saw a police car today and met the sheriff. Daniel says the sheriff here is checking up on us. That's nice," Catherine said, breaking Hannah out of her thoughts.

"It is. They drive by a lot, but I don't want you to bother your sisters about it. Rosemary might get scared if she knows."

Catherine nodded, understanding how her sister would be frightened by the extra security. "Are we safe here, Mom? Like, really safe, like Daniel says?"

"We are." Hannah wanted to believe it was true, but privately she wasn't so sure. First, there was the tire tracks at the mill a week ago, and now a strange man watching them eat ice cream.

"Did you know my name means I will do well when I grow up and my family loves me?"

Hannah smiled. "It is a strong name for a young lady."

"Daniel says I can work at the mill sometimes. Like on a Saturday when he has lots of paperwork, or when school is out. He thinks I'm smarter than Jesse Plank."

"Stay away from those boys who tease you." Hannah moved across the room to collect Catherine's clothes from the floor.

"He said I was freakishly tall and weird because I didn't know we weren't supposed to dress up for Halloween," Catherine said.

"I'm sorry you didn't get to trick-or-treat this year." Hannah would never admit it, but she was glad to be rid of the ritual this year. She never was a fan of Halloween.

"It okay. I didn't want to anyhow. Daniel says Amish *maedels* don't do that and that hitting boys goes against God. But Jesse is going to be punished for being mean to me."

Hannah jerked in surprise. "Is he now?"

"Yep. Daniel won't let boys pick on me anymore, Mom," Catherine said as she yawned.

"Catherine, Daniel is very nice to do and say all of those things, but remember, darling, we won't be here forever." Hannah couldn't let this go on much longer. Now even her most stubborn child was growing attached to Daniel. To this life. Hannah finished hanging Catherine's dress on a peg on the wall and moved back to the bed. "When this is over, we'll find a nice house and start over." Hannah bent down and kissed Catherine's cheek.

"Dad never carried me out of the rain before. We never ate ice cream at a diner either. Was I so bad he didn't love me?"

"Oh, baby, no." Hannah gasped and enveloped her daughter in her arms. "Your father loved you very much. His job was just so important he could never be around as much as other dads."

"But why weren't we more important?" Catherine asked. Hannah knew the answer. She just wasn't sure how to tell her child. How did a mother teach honesty and integrity when she herself had lived a lie for ten years?

Chapter Fifteen

Daniel switched off the gas-powered mill when he saw the buggy approach. He hadn't talked to his *onkel* in a few days and right now he could use a bit of the bishop's wisdom.

"Had a free hour, thought to waste it on you." Joshua winked as he climbed down from the buggy. A light mist had encouraged fog to linger longer than usual. Daniel tethered the old mare to the mill office's porch post and led him inside.

"Looks different in here," his *onkel* observed. Daniel shuffled some papers into a neat stack and pushed them aside on the large desk.

"Catherine is a better organizer than I ever was." A nine-year-old had a better system of life than he did. When had his life become so disorganized? *When the bishop knocked on his door, that's when.*

"It wonders me how you all are." Joshua removed his black felt hat revealing a shiny bald spot on top of his head. "Edith wanted to give you all some space, but I think she is missing spending time with those *kinner* of yours."

"*Nee*, we are managing," Daniel said, unsure. "You needn't worry."

"You are my *schwesder*'s sohn. I will always worry." Joshua grinned. "Any word on this man the law is looking for?" Joshua reached into his pocket and pulled out a handful of mixed hard candies. He offered one to Daniel, who declined. For a man who constantly ate candy, those teeth sure looked healthy.

"They got a few leads. Some people spotted him in Indiana, but there's no word on if it's connected to whoever was sneaking around here."

Joshua raked his thin beard and remained silent.

"I haven't told Hannah all of that. I didn't want her to worry. The *kinner* are doing so well. I would hate to see Rosemary frightened again. The agents and sheriff all know."

"*Jah*, I've seen them driving about regularly. That's *gut*."

"Marshal Bates thinks he didn't even know Rosemary saw him. If she saw him."

His *onkel* shook his head. No one wanted

to see children scared, put in harm's way. "Man is a fickle creature, tending to ignore what is placed in front of him, yet is relentless to have what isn't." He fixed Daniel with a chastised glare. "I will continue to pray for them, and you." Joshua went to the office window and watched the men run lumber through the edger. "Edith is quite taken with that little one."

"I'm quite taken with her myself." Daniel smiled, helpless against it.

"And her *mudder*." Joshua turned and pinned him with a probing look.

"She is Michael's wife, *Onkel*."

"*Nee*, she is Michael's widow. Hannah is your *fraa*. A second chance at a family *Gott* has blessed you with."

"This is all make believe, for safety's sake. Nothing more." His *onkel* wasn't buying it. Daniel tossed a wood-marking pencil aside. "She's been avoiding me for days," he added. What had changed from one day to the next, Daniel hadn't a clue.

"This situation won't always stand between you," Joshua said as he placed his hat back on his barren head. "She has taken to our ways well enough. Edith is going to teach her to sew dresses and coats tomorrow. She has a good start. Maybe she does not feel as you feel. Some come to us seeking a simpler path, one closer to *Gott*."

"She didn't come here willingly," Daniel reminded him. "We are partners, protecting the girls." Daniel lowered his head and angrily added, "Protecting this lie."

The bishop sighed heavily, then asked, "Is it really so hard for you, Daniel?" Daniel narrowed his brows in confusion. "Hard to admit you love your wife? That you're capable of loving? Most men would envy what you two have."

"No man would envy this, *Onkel*. She will leave someday. They all will." Taking his heart along with them.

"Not if you do things right. Haven't you ever considering courting her?"

"My bishop suggests I court my *fraa*?" Daniel laughed out loud at the very thought. "Now that's building the house before cutting the tree."

"I admit we put you in such a position. Your *mudder* loved you, loved you and Michael both. My dear *schwesder*, Martha, had such a kind heart. I see many of those qualities in Hannah." Daniel had too, which was why he was struggling so much. "She loved your *daed* even after he dragged her away from her family and her community. She loved your *bruder* even when he ran away. She wrote me, often. I know everything about him getting in trouble for drinking and stealing and even that time you got taken out of school for fighting."

"You knew about that?" Daniel blurted out. "Well, I didn't know any better then. And the guy would have beaten Michael." Daniel turned toward the window and shook his head. "He liked to start things and I always got stuck cleaning them up afterward."

"This isn't that, Daniel," Joshua assured.

"Feels like it most days." But on other days, it felt like Michael wasn't between them. That it was just him and Hannah and three little girls trying to live a life, one day at a time.

"If you love her, don't compare yourself. I know her life with Michael was not easy. She talks to Edith. I believe he wanted to leave her before he passed." Daniel's fist tightened. Hannah blamed herself, believed she had not been a good enough wife, and here his brother had been considering abandoning her, his children. His veins ran hot in the knowing.

"Michael was never content for long. He never put *Gott* and family before his own selfish wants. If Hannah knew this truth, that you are Michael's *bruder*, she would never think you the lesser man."

"No, she would think me a liar, keeping secrets from her, just as Michael did. She will never understand the full of it. She has been through so much." Daniel stopped. His *onkel* didn't need to hear what he was thinking.

"Then show her how not all men are alike, even those raised under the same roof."

And by showing her, his *onkel* was suggesting Daniel court her. It was ridiculous, a complete contradiction to the order of things, and yet, the very notion of courting Hannah struck a dusty chord in his chest.

A little after two that afternoon, Daniel veered his buggy into the school parking lot. He was early but Catherine burst out the schoolhouse doors and hopped up into the buggy before Daniel could blink. "How was school today?"

"I hate this place," she said angrily folding both arms over her chest.

"*Hate* is a strong word. My day was not so *gut* either." They were both in a foul mood, so instead of turning right toward home, he turned left. "I know what we both need." Twenty minutes later, Daniel watched as Catherine drank her milkshake noisily.

"We just drove a horse through McDonald's drive-through," she busted out laughing and Daniel laughed too.

"I once took Maybelle through a car wash. You should have seen people's faces then." She laughed again, and his heart did somersaults knowing he had a part in that. Without all the hardness, she was a delight. Daniel felt their friendship kindling and hoped she felt it too. No child should feel so alone, without a friend to turn to, without a *daed* to protect her.

"You ran out of there so fast today, I wondered if you didn't punch Jesse right before I showed up, and now I am an accomplice to your crime."

"He won't stop teasing me. I said you're welcome wrong in Amish, and he said I talk funny, and my hair is too short because I can't keep it pinned up right. He said I must have had lice, because they shave your head when you have lice. I couldn't say it wasn't true without him knowing I'm a fake Amish girl."

"I remember my first week of school when we moved to Chicago. I had an older *bruder* so I thought I was safe from such things as teasing." An English school with hundreds of kids had been quite the experience after attending a small two-room Amish schoolhouse.

"I wish I had an older sister," Catherine said solemnly.

"It isn't all wonderful. He got me in more

trouble than I could find alone. He would pick on other kids and start fights. Then I had to pretend to be the big *bruder*."

"Doesn't sound like a very nice brother," Catherine replied.

"He wasn't, but he was mine."

"You weren't mean like that, were you? Like your brother or Jesse?" Her big blue eyes looked up to him.

"*Nee.* One of us had to be responsible." He nudged her. "The eldest is supposed to look out for the youngest, but I loved him and didn't mind, much."

"So it is my job not to make things harder for Rosemary and M.J.?"

"Precisely. You are the eldest and must set a good example, and you are a very wise young *maedel*, Catherine Faith."

"I know." She grinned, cocked her head and smiled. "But Sunday for church, I am not letting him have any of *mudder*'s *kichlin*."

When they reached home, Daniel saw the dark vehicle at the end of his lane. He pulled on the reins, bringing Colt to a stop. The driver's side window rolled down and he recognized the man as one of the two agents who had been there the night Hannah and the girls arrived in his home.

"Hello."

"Mr. Raber," the agent greeted in a sturdy frown. "I'm agent Lawson. I'm here giving the locals a break. I'll be here until sunup, sir, until told otherwise." Lawson's arm rested on the window. His intense gaze told of a man who took his position seriously.

"Come to the house for supper. It's the least we can do for all your help."

"I might take you up on that." Lawson nearly cracked a grin. "There are only so many burgers and cups of stale coffee a man can tolerate."

The agent followed them to the house and Daniel welcomed him inside. "I brought company for supper, Hannah. Hope you don't mind," Daniel said as he entered a kitchen that smelled of tomato sauce and fresh garlic bread.

"Agent Lawson," Hannah said in a surprised voice as the tall man stepped into the room. "Is there any news?"

"No, ma'am. Just keeping watch over everything," Lawson said.

"Well, I'm glad you've come to join us. I hope you like baked spaghetti. The girls have been on me to make it. We have salad too, and an apple cobbler for dessert."

"It sounds wonderful, ma'am. Thank you for inviting me."

As Hannah and Catherine set the table, Daniel helped M.J. into the seat next to him. The agent sat in the empty chair at the far end of the table and once everyone had settled, Daniel lowered his head to commence the silent prayer. After a minute, Daniel cleared his throat, and all heads lifted. Hannah quickly began filling plates for everyone. "So, Mr. Lawson, where are you from, exactly?"

"A native Hoosier," he replied, offering up his plate. For the next half hour, the two of them talked like old friends. They spoke of restaurants they frequented, scenic towns they knew. Daniel began to feel the slow sting of jealousy creep into his gut. Especially since Hannah hadn't once looked his way throughout the meal. He helped M.J. cut her spaghetti into smaller pieces and tried to ignore his unease. Hannah didn't even offer him dessert. Daniel had to spoon out his own serving. Was she punishing him or simply keeping her distance?

After a meal that lasted longer than he wanted, Daniel escorted the agent to the door. He would sleep better tonight knowing someone else was looking out for the family, but he felt like the *Englischer* had worn out his welcome.

"Thanks again for the meal. Magnolia said

she would run out breakfast come daybreak, but I don't see the sense in her going to all the trouble."

"I'll let *Hannah* know. *Gut nacht*." Daniel closed the door and stomped back into the kitchen.

"If you plan on feeding him come morning, it will be me who takes it to him," he said before crossing the room and stomping out the kitchen door to do his evening rounds.

Daniel flipped on the flashlight and made his way toward the barn. Since when had he become possessive and brooding? Hannah of course simply enjoyed talking about home with someone who understood. Daniel shared no history with her, personally. And then he had to go on and act like a jealous *dummkopp*.

At his entrance, the goats all came to life and started bawling. Daniel went to fetch them a scoop of feed to quiet their ruckus.

"I see all of you are enjoying the spoils of the *kinner*." He shined a light on each one and noted just how overly fat they were getting.

"So do you all think I'm an idiot too?" He scooped out another bit of grain and watched as they took right to it. "Well, we might not have history, or anything close to normal," he said tossing the feed scoop back into the grain bin. "But that doesn't mean we can't have a future."

Chapter Sixteen

"I like this daddy. He's funner. He tells stories and thinks my hair is pretty even when it won't stay in my *kapp*." M.J. giggled. "He says my *kapp* can't hold all my pretty in, but I should hide it or some smelly boy might pull my curls."

"Your *daed* is right. Boys can be smelly. Now finish playing with the coloring books I brought you and eat your cake while I show your *mudder* how to cut a dress." Edith stepped into the kitchen where Hannah had already spread out a light green material across the family table.

"This is a nice shade," Hannah complimented. "I have only quilted some, but can't say I know a thing about sewing clothes from scratch."

"It is not so hard," Edith ensured as she began spreading out pattern pieces and explaining them. "Do the *kinner* like the swing Daniel and Joshua hung for them?"

"Yes. They love it." Hannah mimicked tracing a sleeve from her side of the kitchen table. "They play on it nearly every day. I could have saved a lot of money over the years if I'd just hung a swing," Hannah noted.

"You need a sewing machine. I shall speak to Daniel of it."

"Oh, no, please don't. Daniel has done plenty already. I have some money left from Bryan," Hannah said, trying to hold back her anger. Last thing she wanted was something else to owe Daniel for.

"*Nee*, you are not doing the asking, I am," Edith quirked. "I heard Catherine missed school. I hope it was not because of her troubles with Jesse Plank?"

Hannah looked up from the table. "She came home crying the other day and told me that he'd said she had lice. And that was why her hair isn't long like the other girls." She went back to marking material. "Micah always insisted they kept their hair cut short, but I convinced him shoulder-length was best."

"I wonder if that *bu* has any sense at all. Takes after Eli, that one. That man speaks his thoughts aloud more than he ties his own shoes," Edith said, ill-tempered. "That poor *kind.* She has been handed a hard blow. Well, I shall continue to pray for her."

"Daniel took her to work with him recently, then out for ice cream." Hannah looked up from her work. Edith would see how this could be a problem. The woman was keen about others.

"Daniel is a smart man. He has the *kinner*'s best interests at heart. Even so, it is good to see him happy."

"Happy? How is it possible he's so happy? We have disrupted his life completely."

"It is as plain as day you being here has made him happy. Family brings joy, and you would do well to accept that. *Gott* does not mean for us to be alone," Edith said.

"But he will be alone, when we leave. I'm concerned the children are growing too attached to him. I hope they find this guy Corsetti soon. I hate to see my children hurt more than they already have." Hannah looked up and noted Edith's sorrowful expression. "Edith? What is it?"

Edith sniffled. "I'm sorry, my dear. It is just… I would hate to see you go. I have come to care a great deal about you and the *kinner*."

"But this isn't our home. We can't stay and pretend that it is…forever."

"A home is a place where we feel love. You

have been given a second chance to feel love here. So has your *dochdern*. *Gott* does not make mistakes. Does it not feel like you are loved?"

"Feels like straddling a fence," Hannah said. "Like we are neither fully in this world or the English one." She went on. "Besides, Daniel feels obligated to help us. That's all." Hannah reached for a marking pencil. "We are like the guest that never leaves. We have been here almost six weeks."

Edith chuckled. "Time enough. Now you stop all that fretting about what could be and focus on today. You are his *fraa*. Those are his *kinner*. Has he not provided and cared for each of you?"

"Well, yes, but..." They were Micah's children, not Daniel's.

"Have you not in return tended to his home?"

"Mostly but..." But Daniel was only doing what any honorable man would do, tend to his brother's family. Though she had to admit, Micah would have never gone so far for another.

"It is perfectly normal to feel something for Daniel. You two have been good for each other." Edith tilted her head. Hannah let out a sigh. Edith had a gift for seeing what was hid furthest in the heart, and bringing it to the surface. Hannah cared for him and there was no hiding it from his *aenti*.

"There are things you don't know. Things I just discovered about him, and me. It wouldn't be right." Hannah shook her head, wishing they could talk about something else.

"So he told you about Michael, did he?" Edith crossed both arms over her ample chest.

"You knew?" Hannah gasped. Had her closest confidante lied to her, as well? Hannah took a step back. Was no one on this earth trustworthy?

"Of course." Edith waved a hand. "You weren't ready to know. You have endured so much. You lost a husband, your *kinner* were in danger, and you were pulled out of your world and brought to a strange place. All this happened so fast. It was no lie to give you time to gain your footing." Hannah believed her. Edith would never purposely hurt her.

"Daniel doesn't know that I know, but he only agreed to this because of who we are. He thought it was his duty, tending to us as he has. He is an honorable man." The most honorable and amazing man she had ever known. "He cares because we are the only family he has left."

"Maybe at first," Edith quickly agreed.

"Daniel has always had to pick up after Michael. He wanted to help you, but that doesn't mean he doesn't have feelings of his own. The two are not so very different, *jah*?" They were different, Hannah recognized.

"But we come from two totally different worlds."

"*Nee*, you have both known each side of a fence. You are not so different." Edith pinned her with that knowing look. Was Edith right? Daniel had lived in her world and now she lived in his. "It only matters which place holds your heart." That was the problem, Hannah thought. She didn't know where she belonged. What she did know was that Micah was nothing like Daniel, and how she was feeling about him wasn't the same either. But he had withheld the truth from her.

"Your past hardships do not mean you don't deserve love from a good man." It was scary how Edith knew exactly what she was thinking. "*Gott* wants us to give love and receive it. You have that here, with Daniel. You got through all of that, to be here where *Gott* wants you. How do you know that He didn't mold you for this life?"

"I don't know what love is, really. I can't be trusted with such a thing," Hannah murmured as tears threatened.

"Oh, stuff and nonsense. You are a grown woman with three *kinner* whom you have proven you would do anything for. I have no doubts you know what love is. I see it when you look at them." Edith went to her.

"I was a fool, Edith. My choices have already affected my children's lives, forever."

"I see it there, between the lines. I see you holding on to a past that hurts. Worry doesn't fix a thing or complete a single chore. It just gives us wrinkles in all the wrong places. Do you still love Michael so much your heart has no room for another?"

"I was so young, so eager for love, a family. I thought he loved me, believed he did… at first. I thought he knew me. He told me that his life had been similar to mine. I thought we shared that connection, that he understood me. I let him have my heart without stopping to think if I wanted to give it away so easily." The tears were unleashed.

"Ach, mei lieb." Edith held her hand.

"He didn't want children and I…" she laughed through her sobs "…wanted them so desperately. When Catherine was born, he was angry, but he got over it. But when I got pregnant with Rosemary, he thought I was doing it to make his life harder."

"Some men feel pressures us women can

never understand," Edith said. "Their father was like this. My poor Joshua spent many a day begging him to change his ways. Martha Jane had a hard life married to that one."

Martha Jane, M.J. Hannah felt the air slip out of her. Had her daughter been given the very name of her grandmother? Daniel and Micah were two very different people. How had God made two brothers, born of the same house, so different? Micah was full of sweet charms and selfish wants. Daniel rarely spoke and hadn't a selfish bone in his body.

"Dan took them away from us, to the *Englisch* world, because he couldn't submit to *Gott*. He liked to drink and smoke, and I think Joshua feared he had a gambling habit, as well. It broke poor Martha's heart. You should know those *kinner* have the look of her. I saw it plain as day the first time I laid eyes on them." Was that what had drawn Daniel in so deeply with her daughters? "Martha was a gentle heart. Very giving. She would have loved meeting her *grosskinner*. Did Michael ever speak of her?"

"Never. He told me he had no family." Hannah lowered her head. "He lied, about everything. The girls, they needed him. They needed him to make them feel safe, loved. Make them feel like they mattered." She turned to Edith again. "He never bought them ice cream or let them have pets or read them stories at night. He never loved us."

"Not like Daniel."

"Daniel gave Rosemary the bees and M.J. the sun. He made Catherine smile, and reads books with her. They love him. They beg for his attention and…"

"He gives it. Because that is what fathers do." Edith touched her shoulder. "My heart hurts to know you lived a life such as this, but that does not mean you should accept that as the way life should be for your *kinner. Gott* loves you and you have a home here if you want it."

"I don't matter. It's the girls who do. Plus, I'm not even Amish. Even if that was a possibility, I can't."

"There are steps to be taken, *jah*. It wonders me if you want to know what those are." Edith smiled cunningly. Hannah wasn't sure what she wanted, but she knew being a burden on another man wasn't it. The front door slammed shut and Hannah jerked away, rushing to wipe the tears from her face.

"Why do I feel my ears burning?" Daniel teased as he walked into the room. Hannah turned her back to him and busied herself placing the cut-out pattern over the material. She couldn't let him see her crying, or asking questions. Catherine moved toward her.

"How was school today?"

"It was not good," Catherine said. Then she looked to Daniel and smiled. "But it got better. We had shakes and Daniel says I get my own pay for working at the mill."

"He did, did he?" Edith arched a brow. Hannah turned slightly and smiled at her daughter.

"Daniel, your *fraa* needs a sewing machine," Edith blurted out to Hannah's embarrassment.

"Then she shall have one. It would be good for the girls too. If you have plans on using it," he tested, looking to Hannah. She watched his smile fade when he caught sight of her teary eyes.

"I really don't think we will need one. It would be a waste of money considering we won't be here long enough to enjoy it." With that Hannah hurried from the room, putting as much distance between her and Daniel as possible. Pretending to love a man was just as hard as truly loving him.

The air grew chilly, and there was a hint of snow threatening. Daniel stoked the fire in the fireplace, and could tell from the sounds of things that Hannah was having trouble getting the girls to bed tonight. Putting the poker down, he climbed the stairs and went to tuck Rosemary in while Hannah wrangled M.J. into bed. They would have to be more careful how many sweets that one devoured after supper.

"Danki," Rosemary whispered as Daniel pulled an extra quilt from the chest at the end of her bed.

"I'm proud of you for sleeping in your own room." He unfolded the quilt.

"I can't be a baby forever. And I know there is a police car driving by the house a lot. So I'm not afraid."

"Have you said your prayers?"

"Yes. I like it here. I like Colt and milking Daisy. Did M.J. tell you she wants a cat?" Rosemary smiled.

"Jah, she did." Daniel smiled in return, then sat on the edge of her bed. "And that she named all the goats after princesses."

She was doing so well adjusting to life here. Far from the mute, frightened little girl he met on that dark September night several weeks ago.

"I think she would want a dog, an elephant and maybe a monkey if I allowed it." He leaned down, kissed her forehead and got to his feet again. "Need me to leave the lamp on longer?"

"I can see with the big moon outside. Daniel…" she paused "…I know *Aenti* Edith says we should call you *Daed* when we have visitors."

"*Jah.*" He held his breath.

"Can I call you *Daed* here too?"

"*Jah*, Rosemary. I would like that very much. *Gut nacht, liebling.*" Daniel fought back his emotions. Little girls needed to feel that the men in their life were strong, but right now he felt like a melted puddle of goo. He slipped into the hall, pulled Rosemary's door near shut, and there stood Hannah, her eyes brimming with tears.

Suddenly, she turned on a heel and ran down the stairs. He chided himself for not telling her about Rosemary speaking before making his own way downstairs to deal with the situation.

She stood in the family room, staring at the fire, red and orange dancing with each other. "How long…how long has she been talking to you?" Her voice was full of pain.

"Not long."

She spun angrily. "How…? Why…?" If one ever doubted she could be fury and backbone, all they had to do was see Hannah right now. At that moment, nothing soft or vulnerable existed. He had done that to her.

"I'm sorry, Hannah. I should have told you the first time it happened. I have no excuse.

She is only now comfortable with it. I had hoped she would have opened up to everyone sooner, on her own, but…"

"But she trusts you."

"It was an accident, I think. She was upset one day and just blurted out a few words." He edged cautiously closer. "She worries about you, about more than little girls should. I'm sorry." Daniel would do anything to show just how sorry he was.

"I'm being selfish." She straightened her shoulders and lifted her chin.

"*Nee*, you are her mother. It is me who was selfish. I had no right. Rosemary is your daughter and…"

"And she is your niece." Daniel jerked to attention. How did she know? His heart dropped like a heavy stone into the bottom of his gut.

"I'm right, aren't I? Micah is…was… Michael and you are…his brother?" Daniel clenched his jaw but said nothing. "You kept secrets and lied to me." Hannah brushed the tears from her face and stormed past him.

Daniel reached out, took her arm to stop her. No more lies, no more pretending. "How did you know?"

Like that evening on the porch, she reached out to touch the scar no longer visible on his neck. "This. Micah told me that story. He loved

Indiana Jones. And that dog. He painted that dog because your deacon reported him for smoking." His gaze landed on her eyes, the pain he'd added there. "He said his family was dead. It was just one of his many lies. He said you all abandoned him and then died. How could you not tell me?"

"Bates said it was safer not to. I wanted to, Hannah. I only found out about Michael, about his family, hours before you showed up at my door. You weren't the only one hurt and having to make decisions quickly."

"You knew this and still, you almost kissed me." The pain on her face was unbearable.

"I hope you can forgive me for that too. It won't happen again." How many mistakes was he going to keep making?

"You took us in because he was your brother. You felt obligated in taking care of his burdens. You are both made from the same cloth and it's woven together with nothing but lies." She jerked away from him but Daniel held firm.

He was selfish, like Michael, because he wanted something he could never possibly have. He wanted her. Daniel loosened his hold on her arm, but didn't let go completely. "I did what I thought was best…for you and your girls. My obligations have changed. I have my own reasons now." *Stupid Daniel.*

"And they are?" She stiffened.

"Those *kinner* up there sleeping." He pointed toward the stairs.

"I hate that they love you, even Catherine, though she would never admit it."

Her tone grew softer, less cutting. But did she love him? That's what Daniel wanted to know. Could she ever move past the mistakes of his family, see him as someone worthy of her? Could she forgive that he'd kept so many things from her?

They were close, a breath away. His other hand brushed a tendril of hair behind her ear. "I love them too," he admitted, his heart pounding in his chest. He needed to close the chasm between them. He'd worked so hard building that bridge and felt as if he was losing that now. Daniel couldn't let that happen.

So before she could utter another harsh word, he kissed her. And to his surprise, she kissed him back. Hannah melted into him and everything that stood between them vanished. He was the first to pull away and missed her immediately.

"I'm sorry." She looked breathless, stunned. Both good signs that he hadn't burned that bridge. Relief washed over him.

"Me too." Even in firelight the blush on her cheeks was apparent.

"I should…"

"Get some rest," he quickly said, noting her dazed state. He watched her retreat back upstairs wishing he'd said something more. What he wanted was to kiss her again, but Daniel had surprised her plenty for one evening. And a kiss like that left a person a lot to think about. She needed time to think after his boldness. They both did.

Picking up the poker, he gave the fire a little stir and added another large log to keep for the night. Hannah had fit into his life and without knowing it, gave him a glimpse of what family truly meant. She thought him the expert, but it was her, in all her selfless love and fierce determination. No matter her plight, Hannah never quit. Daniel only hoped he could convince her not to start now.

Chapter Seventeen

Hannah managed to keep to herself the next few days and Daniel didn't show any signs of caring she did. Neither knew how to handle that unexpected kiss. Nor how to deal with such strong feelings that followed. At least Rosemary was speaking to her now. It was the highlight of Hannah's night, tucking her into bed, saying prayers together. Her daughter was healing, and surprisingly Hannah was too.

Until that kiss. She knew he regretted it, letting the moment seize his common sense, but it was making things difficult for her. She couldn't stop thinking about him.

She finished washing up and pinned on a clean dress and apron before going downstairs. She'd promised the girls they could play on the porch. As she began working out the tangles in her wet hair, Hannah stared out the kitchen window. The cool breeze of the season twirled up anything outside not rooted in the earth, but she felt nothing but warmth in this house and life that Daniel had made for himself— and for them.

"Mommy!" M.J. came bursting into the kitchen, her *kapp* lopsided, her new coat unlatched. "Princess Fiona is dying!"

"Martha Jane, I told you not to go outside or to the barn without me or Daniel with you." She would have to nail M.J.'s dress to the floor to keep her close.

"We were on the porch. You said the porch was fine." Knowing Agent Lawson and the county sheriff were just down the lane, keeping watch, Hannah thought the porch was perfectly safe. "She's under the tree swing, dying. Mommy help her. Don't let Princess Fiona die." Her daughter produced real tears, something she rarely succumbed too. Hannah tossed her brush onto the counter and rushed outside to see what the fuss was all about.

Just as her daughter said, under the large oak in the front yard, lay Princess Fiona. The black nanny goat was lying on her side, her stomach twice its normal size. Hannah knelt beside her. "What have you got into?" A thousand scenarios ran through her mind. Poisonous plants she didn't know of, or maybe she had gotten into the feed and overeaten. Wasn't that what Daniel called founder? It wasn't until the nanny began to push that it became crystal clear what was happening.

"Catherine," she yelled toward the porch where Rosemary and Catherine stood. "Fetch a bucket of fresh water by the pump." Catherine bolted around the house without hesitating. "Rosemary, get a couple towels from the line." Like her eldest daughter, Rosemary didn't pause.

"Is she gonna die, Mommy?" M.J. whimpered.

"No, sweetie." Hannah smiled up to her daughter. "She is going to be a mommy."

M.J.'s eyes lit up. "A mommy? For real?" Hannah was just as surprised. Daniel fussed the girls were overfeeding the goats and making them into spoiled pets. He would be in for quite a shock when he returned home today.

"Now rub her head and talk to her like you do any other day. It will help keep her calm." Hannah wished Daniel were here, but after bringing Catherine home from school, he had a couple more hours before he left the mill for the day. It was cold and windy, the ground still slightly damp from misting most of the day, but Hannah knew it was too late to persuade the cantankerous animal to move into the barn.

"Well, Princess Fiona, let's have a baby." Hannah tucked her damp hair behind her ears and rolled up her sleeves.

At first, Daniel suspected Hannah had killed the old pesky goat, but when Rosemary stood cradling something with four dangling legs, he knew. *Just what I needed, more pets for M.J. to give silly names to.* He looked heavenward before letting out a hearty laugh.

When he neared them, all four females beamed, but it was a set of blue eyes sparkling with sweet wonder that held him transfixed. Hannah carried a second black kid wrapped in a towel toward him in a proud stride.

"A boy. Well, two boys actually. Now we know why she was so moody." She laughed, her eyes sparking with life and enthusiasm he had never seen before. Her hair was partly damp, the wind playing with the strands. And he knew right then in that moment—Magnolia Reynolds was a woman born to a world that tried molding her to its own selfish way. She all but said so. But Hannah Raber was happy and he knew it took so little to give that to her. How had such a big world failed her he hadn't a clue, but he had every intention of giving her all that he had.

"Well—" he reached out and patted the kid's

head, still warm and damp to the touch "—
me and Colt *were* feeling outnumbered. We
needed a few more males around here." A gust
of wind sent his hat tumbling away. Catherine
hurried to fetch it.

"You three want to help move them to the
barn before milking?" he asked, still focused
on Hannah, the way her hair danced about her
beautiful features.

"Milking is done." She titled her head and
floated him a proud smile. That same smile
she'd given him when Millie and Margaret had
arrived unannounced at his door. She wasn't
angry anymore.

"Well then, *fraa*, thank you." He winked at
her before heading toward the barn. Life was
shifting and Daniel was glad it was.

Chapter Eighteen

There was something about a Thursday that always made Daniel uneasy. He'd left Kentucky for the *Englisch* world on a Thursday. And had returned to it on a Thursday. He'd become a husband and father on a Thursday too, and this cold November morning the wind woke him, warning him another shift was coming.

He slipped downstairs to make *kaffi* and add fresh wood on the fire so the children woke to warm floors. The house was quiet. He thought he would miss that, but was growing accustomed to the sounds of feet running across the upper hall, giggles that made concentration impossible and the sweet strawberry scent of Hannah's shampoo wafting from room to room.

He discovered Hannah was already up, moving about, lamplight illuminating her small curvy frame as she reached into the fridge and pulled out bacon and eggs and milk. She stilled, sensing him near, and when she turned to smile his way, Daniel wanted to kiss her just like he had before. He loved her, and he couldn't deny it anymore.

"Gut morgen."

"Gut morgen." Her soft voice made him smile inside. He thought about just how much he wanted to wake up to mornings just like this one. Every morning. "Coffee?"

"Jah, danki." Daniel lifted both suspenders over his shoulders as he watched her retrieve a cup from the cabinet nearby and begin filling it. He took a seat at the table, careful not to let it scrape the floor, waking the children. Getting up early had been instilled in him since childhood, but the girls didn't need to get used to it. They would soon leave, back to a life where 7:00 a.m., and not 4:30 a.m., was normal. "I'll see to the morning milking today. It's getting colder out."

"I don't mind. I think I'm finally getting the hang of it." She turned his direction. "As long as M.J. is there to talk Daisy through my tortures," Hannah laughed softly. She carried him over a cup, then turned back to start breakfast when he said nothing more. They were both stalling. Neither willing to discuss what was going on between them. He watched as she placed bacon in the cast-iron skillet, turned on the heat of the gas stove. He wanted to ask her to stay, but feared her answer. The thought of her leaving, the children leaving, was tearing him apart. He was committed to this life, this marriage. If she would only acknowledge that kiss, say something to give him a reason to hope, he could tell her. One thing Hannah had few of was choices. He wanted this choice to be hers.

The silence lingered longer than he could stand. Daniel drank down his coffee and silently sat his cup aside. As much as he loved the idea of simply sitting there, watching her as she began mixing ingredients for biscuits, he knew that was only going to torture him further. He carefully rose, retrieved his coat and hat from the third peg by the door, and slipped out in the cold dark morning.

Maybe that kiss didn't mean to her what it had to him after all.

Daniel's bones ached like a January night as he sawed log after log. Why hadn't he told her how he felt this morning? Because she was clearly leaving, that's why. She'd never asked for this life, the Plain life. How could he ask her to give up her world and become Amish?

The sheriff's car pulled up to the mill office. Daniel let Eli take over things and went to greet him. "Afternoon, Sheriff Corbin," Daniel said, drawing close. The sheriff had come to town from somewhere farther south a few years ago. Not quite forty, and an inch taller than Daniel, he looked more like a man who worked the fields than one who rode around in a patrol car all day. The sheriff was friendly, only serious when the need called for it, and was capable of maintaining a peaceful community that was half Amish, half English.

"Your marshal friend called the station this morning." Corbin removed his hat, running a wide palm over his short-cropped head. Daniel ushered him inside the office for privacy. Eli and Vernon would only assume he came to discuss the tire tracks from days ago.

"This Nicholas Corsetti fella is here, in town," Corbin told him.

"I should get back to the house then. The bishop's wife is there with Hannah and the two little ones. How do they know for sure?" Daniel felt his heart begin to race.

"Hotel manager over in Mason reported an out-of-towner taking up a room for about nine days there. Their sheriff's department didn't care much, but when the man called again yesterday, he claimed Room Service had complained about the man. Said he had a gun on him. They called it in, along with the description of the car, plates and the man's description. He checked out, but when they ran the information—" Corbin shook his head "—the car was registered to a man from Ohio. That man was found dead two weeks ago. It seems everything leads to this Corsetti fella."

"Bates had one man already here. Agent Lawson. Besides you, he drives by every so often, came to the house a couple evenings for a meal."

"Yeah, I met him. He sleeps over at the bed-and-breakfast."

"I should go fetch Catherine from school." Daniel moved toward the door. "Can you go to the house until I get there?"

"Sure, you want me to get the girl so you can get home?"

"*Nee*, that will only scare Catherine, and a sheriff's car pulling up to the Amish school might start a panic and stir up questions."

"I've got two deputies now. Once you get back, I'll see Brown sits on the porch round the clock."

"I'm sure Bates will see there are a few agents nearby too. *Danki*, Sheriff." Daniel reached for his hand.

"None required. You're one of ours, now

they are too. No one is getting to them while I'm sheriff here."

Daniel prayed he was right.

Daniel pulled into the small gravel parking lot of the Amish school, a large gray building he had helped build himself. The school had indoor plumbing, three classrooms and a small dining area. The last time Daniel had been inside was last year's Christmas recital. He tethered the horse to one of the six posts and climbed down. Daniel waved at Silas Graber's new bride. She was often carting Silas's two boys to school, but Daniel suspected young Aiden was getting big enough to take on the responsibility soon. It was clear love had been kind to them all and her rounded frame said the former widower was better at crossing rivers and building bridges than Daniel was.

He stepped into the front door. "Daniel?" He looked over to Lydia Ann Byler, Catherine's teacher, a stack of papers in her hands, dodging out of a room to the left.

"Why are you here?" Her head tilted in confusion.

"To pick up *mei dochder*." Daniel met her with equal perplexity.

"But Catherine never attended today," Lydia

said, her eyes growing wider as the words left her.

"I dropped her off, right here," Daniel said, his voice doing nothing to conceal his growing panic.

"Oh, my." Lydia's hands flew to her mouth. "Daniel, she hasn't been here all day. I thought you kept her home again. Oh, Daniel…" But he heard no more as he raced his buggy to the nearest phone a half mile away. Daniel called 911, then Bates.

News traveled fast in Amish communities. Before Hannah had a chance to grasp what the sheriff was saying, the sound of several buggies clattered up the lane. "I will never stop being amazed at how fast the Amish grapevine works," Sheriff Corbin said, shaking his head as he opened the front door. Hannah stepped out onto the porch, her vision blurring. A warm hand touched her shoulder, moved slowly down her back. Was Daniel fearful she would collapse as half of Miller's Creek began filling up the driveway?

"Is this because of my daughter missing?"

"Jah," Daniel said softly behind her. "They will all come to help and won't leave until we find her." She turned to face him.

"They will know, Daniel. They might already know," she said. He reached for her hand, a warm reminder that she wasn't alone.

"Only that our daughter is missing. And that we need their help." When he looked down on her with those serious hazel eyes, a slight wrinkle between them, Hannah knew Catherine's chances were better. Daniel was holding back anger, fury and fear, but that raw determination was right there in those eyes. Amish or not, she had no doubt he would do whatever it took to find Catherine and bring her home safely.

"We lied to them," she said softly. "Why would they want to help me find her?"

"They know why. Even *Gott* knows why. These people love her—and you. We won't stop until she's home."

Warmth filled her. His words stronger than the November chill. "You *will* find her, won't you?"

"Daniel." The sheriff broke between them. "That agent has a man missing but the vehicle has just been spotted not far from here." Corbin bounded off the steps, motioned to a deputy nearby and started giving orders.

"Joshua will see to getting everyone organized. I'm going with him. I will bring her home." Daniel kissed her before running after the sheriff.

"Oh, Hannah, we just heard someone has taken Catherine. I called as many as I could." Millie bound up the steps first, all three of her redheaded girls jumping out of the buggy and running behind her. Millie pulled Hannah into her arms, tears pouring from her face. Hannah looked over Millie's shoulder as Daniel climbed into the sheriff's car. Their eyes held until the car turned away and raced past buggies still arriving. She needed to trust now more than ever.

"You came," she cried into Millie's shoulder.

"We all came. It's what friends do," Millie replied.

Chapter Nineteen

"The agent said they had him cornered just down the road from your mill," the sheriff said over the sirens blaring. "He's on foot now, and she wasn't in the vehicle." Daniel's heart hammered in his chest. Had he already hurt her?

The car pulled into the mill lot where two large black vehicles and a deputy's car were already parked. Five men stood, guns drawn. Another man stepped out of the office, indicating Catherine wasn't inside. Daniel jumped out of the sheriff's car.

"Stay in the car, Daniel, and let us do our job."

"We think she is on foot and he's chasing after her," Lawson said, a smear of blood on his forehead. "Tracks go this way."

"Browning, you stay here with Daniel, call in Search and Rescue and have them standing by. I can't have them entering the woods with an armed man and we don't have enough deputies to escort them right now." The sheriff looked to Daniel. "We have to have him in custody before letting them search, sorry." Daniel appreciated the information but he wasn't happy about it. Catherine was out there, somewhere, waiting for him to come get her.

"She knows the woods here. She might be heading home," Daniel put in. Catherine was smart, he reminded himself. She paid attention to details and Daniel had taken them all through the small wooded area on walks twice now. Besides the mill, she would want to go home, where it's safe, where she would think he was. He believed that in his heart.

Bates ordered a female agent back to the house, just in case. Daniel fought between staying put and rushing home. The agent was in a vehicle and pulling away before he could choose, making the decision for him.

Daniel watched the men all spread out and move into the forest. Browning, the sheriff's deputy remaining behind, turned to him. "They said she jumped from the vehicle and fled into the woods. Don't worry, Mr. Raber, you got a smart, tough girl. They'll find her." His assurances didn't help matters. Daniel knew she wouldn't give up without a fight. Some parts of Michael he was blessed to know she possessed, but there was a fifty-fifty chance this hired gun man would find her first.

"*Gott*, let them find her. Let her find her way home. Let this man be stopped, here and now."

The agent motioned for Daniel to get down and Daniel quickly hid behind the sheriff's car. Movement stirred between lumber stacks. The deputy squatted down in front of him. "Fastest answered prayer I've ever been privileged to witness. Stay here."

"Wait." Daniel reached out to stop him. "Look." Just under the eave of his mill shed, a faint flash of blue caught his eye. "She's hiding above the mill, in the rafters." Daniel's breath exhaled in relief. Now all he had to do was get to her before the gunman did.

"He's looking for her. I'll go around, try to flank him. You know how to use a gun?" The agent started to pull a second weapon from under his coat. Daniel looked around quickly. He spied a nice-sized stacking timber close by.

"*Nee*, I don't need one," Daniel replied. He hoped he would never have to be put in the position to take a life, but fear for Catherine, coupled with knowing if this man got away he would forever threaten his family, he wasn't sure what he would do if the moment presented itself. He had taken his vows to *Gott*, believed them, but in that moment, Daniel knew he would defend life if he was forced to.

The deputy slithered along the car, looked out and ran toward the office. Daniel watched as a few seconds later he made a run for a pile of logs to shield behind. He was edging closer to the killer while Catherine clung to the rafters, hoping not to be seen.

Daniel peeked over the car's hood, the killer, a small light-haired man in jeans, worked his way around another stack of lumber. He was getting closer to the mill, closer to Catherine. Daniel slid the short four-by-four used for stacking lumber off the ground from his right and gripped it tightly. "Please don't put me in this position, but forgive me if I do what I must to save her," he whispered before making a run toward the lumber piles.

"Come out, little one," the killer called out. "Just want to know what your sister knows. Give yourself up and I promise I won't hurt her. Be a good big sister now, come out here."

Daniel steeled his breathing, though his veins pumped rapidly. The deputy had worked his way toward the lumber stacks. Daniel positioned himself opposite the killer. He could no longer see Browning, knowing he was closing in on the murderer, but Daniel couldn't see the killer either, just hear his steps carelessly stomping closer.

"If I take you in, they won't want her. You would be saving your sister."

Heart pounding in his chest, Daniel lifted the stacking timber, tightened his grip. Catherine would indeed give herself up for Rosemary. He knew she would. He couldn't give her time to do that.

"I see you," the monster's voice echoed out. "Nice hiding spot, Jasmine. Your daddy would be proud."

Catherine's voice made a faint cry as the deputy burst out of hiding. "Hold it! You're under arrest!" A shot rang out and Daniel let instincts take over good sense, stepping into the aisle. The killer's back was to him, not two feet away. His gun raised, but no dead deputy lay on the ground ahead. Daniel breathed a quick relief that Browning's agility had saved his life.

"Her name is Catherine," Daniel said. Nick Corsetti turned and Daniel swung as hard as he could, making contact and knocking the man hard into the lumber. He fell down, but before Daniel could react, the deputy was already on top of Corsetti, hitting his gun away.

"Nicolas Corsetti, you are under arrest

for the murders of Micah Reynolds, Charles Brown and Nina Sanchez." The agent looked up to him. "Nice swing, Amish. Go get your daughter." Daniel didn't have to be told twice. Dropping the wooden weapon, he sprinted to Catherine.

"Come on down, Catherine." Daniel reached up into the rafters as Catherine eased down into his arms. He didn't give her a chance to speak before he enveloped her in the safety of his arms.

"I'm sorry, *Daed*. I…"

"Shh. You are here, safe. That is all that matters." He held her for nearly two more minutes before sitting her down and checking for wounds. "Did you hurt yourself getting away?"

Nodding that she was, Catherine looked up at him with those wide blue eyes full of fear and tears. "You came for me," she cried out and he swept her back into his arms again.

"I will always come for you," he promised. "Nobody hurts my *maedel*."

Twenty minutes later, EMS had seen to Catherine while Nick Corsetti was being hauled off in the back of an SUV.

"I would put ice on that knee, maybe take some Tylenol, but surprisingly she's got nothing but bumps and bruises," the female paramedic informed him. "You are one brave little girl." Catherine shrugged.

"I know you're mad," she said, looking to Daniel.

"I'm thankful you are okay."

"But you're mad too. I see it."

"*Nee*, but you scared us half to death, Catherine. Why did you run off from school and let yourself get put in this position?"

"Why do I have to go to school when we are leaving?" She brushed away a few tears and tried looking angry. "Mom said we couldn't stay. So why? Why should I put up with Jesse Plank and his friends or the baby goats? Why should I care if I learn how to sew or make apple pies and muck stalls?" She slapped a hand on her leg. "Why should I help at the mill, counting footages and adding numbers? Why should I like you even if you save me from bad guys if we are leaving?" Then she burst into another run of tears.

"I'll let you two have a moment," the paramedic said, leaving them inside the ambulance alone. Daniel pulled her onto his lap, fighting a rush of tears of his own. He held her a moment longer, felt his heart break in two, before forcing her to look at him.

"Do you want to stay here and muck stalls and play with baby goats instead of hanging out in malls and watching your favorite shows?" He wanted to give her a choice, something none of them had been given so far.

"*Jah*, I do." Her teary blue eyes begged him. "I don't want to go back. I want this to be our home. We like it here, except for Jesse Plank. Everyone loves us. He never loved us," she said on a fresh run of sobs. In the distance, Sheriff Corbin leaned on his car, talking on his phone. Daniel knew he was telling Hannah that Catherine had been found and was safe.

"Your *daed* loved you, Catherine. Michael, I mean, Micah, just loved differently. It doesn't seem fair at nine, but I promise you. He loved you and one day you will understand that he did."

"You don't do…different like he did," she said bluntly. The truth of her nine-year-old wisdom tore a path down the center of his heart. Daniel knew Michael had loved his children, just as their father had loved him and Michael. He also knew that sometimes words weren't always enough. It was action, assurances that children needed to feel that love. Doing the right thing, even when you didn't want to. That's what made a father a father.

"No, *liebling*, I don't. But that doesn't mean he didn't love you."

"Can you make her let us stay? If you're

married, can't you make her? Dad made her do things his way. Can't you *make* her?" Her plea bore desperation.

"That's not how marriage is. I can't force her to do anything, but I could try to convince her you are happy here." Daniel smiled. He'd never imagined this was a life any of them truly wanted.

"How do you know so much?" She wiped her face.

"Not sure about much," he chuckled. "But I understand you. I was nine when we left here and moved to Chicago." He rubbed her back in slow circles as she listened. "I know what it's like not to fit in someplace."

"Did you hate the city too?"

"*Jah*, I hated it. So loud and busy. People weren't very kind. I lived in a small house with my parents and brother, crammed between two other small houses. My parents ran a small store. School in your world is even scarier than here," he noted.

"Where are they now? Your mom and dad and brother? Do I have grandparents? We never had grandparents before."

"They are all gone, but I know Edith would gladly be your *grossmammi*." He watched but her expression didn't waver. Catherine was absorbing it all. It was what she did, considering her words carefully. It was a trait he liked to think she'd gained from him.

"You lost your family?" she asked, shivering against the cold.

"I did." Daniel removed his coat and wrapped her in it.

"But we are your family now, aren't we?"

"You are, and I thank *Gott* every day for bringing you all into my life. I love you, Catherine."

"I love you too, Daniel. I'm sorry I got in that man's car and you had to save me. He said he worked with Bryan and I thought he was here to take care of us. He didn't know Rosemary wasn't in school. If he was watching over us, he would know that, right?"

"Right." Daniel smiled. *As smart as her mother.* "Just never get into a car again." He pulled her close again, breathed in the soft scent of sawdust and little girl.

"I won't."

"Wait, how did you get out of his car?" Daniel asked. Surely she hadn't done as the deputy suggested.

"When he slowed down, I jumped,"she said as if it meant nothing. Daniel wasn't sure his heart was up for the challenge of Catherine Raber in five years from now.

"How about we get back to the house, so

your *mudder* can see you are all right. We will keep this conversation to ourselves for now, but I will talk to her."

"Promise?" she asked.

"Promise." And Daniel never broke a promise.

Chapter Twenty

Daniel leaned against the kitchen counter as Hannah cradled Catherine on her lap. He would never know the gift he had given her this day. She was blessed to have all her children here with her, safe. Bryan told her about the arrest and the fact she had no home to go back to. The bank had already foreclosed and sold it without her there to try to make amends for Micah's debts. She didn't care.

Everything she cared about sat in this very room. Her favorite room of all the rooms she had in a lifetime. This kitchen, though plain, brought her more joy than any other. This is where she came when she woke each morning, prepared meals she had always wanted to. The long table was where she learned to cut dress patterns, how to make the perfect crust and where her family gathered together each day.

The fridge ran on propane, had no ice maker installed and yet held the fresh milk she had gathered from the cow her daughter loved like a best friend. Her favorite pan sat on the back of the stove, waiting for her to make use of it.

"We can see about setting you and the girls up someplace nice. I think it's best you don't return or use your old names in case Marotta finds a reason not to believe Nick's confession."

"But it's almost Thanksgiving," Catherine blurted out.

"*Aenti* Edith and Millie and everyone is coming," M.J. added. "We can't miss the big Thanksgiving with our new family, can we?" M.J. looked to Hannah and put on one of her signature pouts. Gott *bless these two*, Daniel nearly said aloud.

Hannah looked to Daniel. She was waiting for his reaction, not those of the faces around her. "I think missing Thanksgiving would be terrible too. It's just a few days away, and I have been looking forward to your dressing and gravy," he reasoned, hoping to buy more time. In fact, the longer he thought about it, Thanksgiving, which was a Thursday, would be the perfect time to tell her how he felt.

Her damp blue eyes widened in surprise. Daniel noted her fingers were slightly trembling, but before she could grab hold of her apron front to steady them, Rosemary reached up, grasping hold of one of her hands.

"A few more days," the soft voice pleaded. How could the woman not know he wanted her to stay? Even her children knew. He wanted to tell her right then, but not with so many eyes upon them.

"Can we do that?" Hannah looked to Bryan.

"It's your call, Mags. Nobody can answer that but you. You are free to come and go as you please, just keep the identities for now. If you choose to want newer ones, all you have to do is ask." Bryan took a sip of the coffee she had prepared for them while deputies and agents nibbled on sandwiches the women had laid out.

"I think the children and I would like to stay for Thanksgiving if Daniel doesn't mind."

She was clutching to every last minute and it made his heart swell knowing so. "You know I don't. And we have much to be thankful for." His eyes twinkled as he looked over the girls' faces.

"And you promised to make the turkey," Edith put in. "I'm not making all the desserts and the turkey too."

"We do have a lot to be thankful for. We are blessed our Catherine is safe." Millie placed an arm around Hannah's shoulders. "We are blessed with friends and love big enough to fill this room. You can't leave all of that." She couldn't and didn't know how she was going to after Thanksgiving either.

Hannah straightened. It was settled then. Another couple days, she would relish in it. Then she would decide where to go. She looked across the room at the man who taught her not all men were the same. The man who saved her daughter, and her. Edith's words rang in her ears. Daniel would always consider their marriage legal, and now she would too.

"Yeah!" M.J. yelled and jumped into Daniel's arms. "We get to stay. I like it." Daniel chuckled at her signature adage. "I need to go tell Daisy we are staying for Thanksgiving. And I get to milk a goat. This is the best day ever." She squealed.

"Milk a goat," Daniel said, taken aback.

"You said you can milk goats if they become mommies. Well, Princess Fiona is a mommy and she's my size."

Daniel shook his head. "I guess I did."

"You should join us," Hannah spoke to Bryan. Bryan was a friend, more than that. He had brought her here, where she and her children could heal. In that healing, Hannah had found herself, her true self, in the last place she would have ever looked. This Plain world, she was made for. It taught her the value of community, friends and faith. She thought she knew God before, but now she felt closer to Him. Whatever His will was for her, she would obey. She would adapt. But she would never forget Daniel, the man who held her heart.

"I have to escort Corsetti back. No rest or holidays for my kind," Bryan chuckled and gave Catherine a shoulder pat. "But you all take your time, enjoy your holiday and call me once you know what you want to do. And no more getting into cars with strangers, kiddo." Catherine gave him her promise. He gave Hannah a long hug as they said their goodbyes.

Daniel couldn't help but notice the sly grin on Catherine's lips. He had a promise to uphold, and he would. Just a couple more days, because no longer would Thursdays break him.

Daniel walked the marshal and his men to the door. "Take good care of them," Bates said over a shoulder.

"I intend to." Daniel watched the vehicles, one by one, disappear over the east rise. Catherine was safe. The children were safe. He blew out a breath.

It was late at night before the last buggy pulled out of the drive. Daniel lifted Rosemary from his lap, her sleepy head rolling into his chest. "I should put this one down."

"Thank you, Daniel," Hannah said, turning from the sink. "I know what you did. Thank you for saving her."

"She saved herself," he replied. "I just happened to be there to notice," he said modestly.

"Will you read to us tonight?" M.J. asked.

"I would love to."

Chapter Twenty-One

A house full of females. Daniel never imagined he would one day have a house full of females, or that he would be happy about it. His mother would be laughing right now, a big smile on her face. In his mind's eye, he could see her gray eyes gleaming with joy, knowing her home was filled with family, with abundant love.

Millie, Hannah and Millie's older two daughters were elbow-deep in the kitchen, finishing the last of the meal. The women had grown close and had more in common than being widows and mothers. Their bond was sisterly, and it warmed Daniel's heart that Hannah was receiving a forever love of a sister she had never had before.

His *onkel* Joshua took it upon himself to carve the turkey that looked just about perfect. Hannah's cooking skills never ceased to amaze him.

He slipped outside for some fresh air. Sitting in the swing on the porch, he watched the children chase the two little goats around the yard. Ivy, Millie's youngest daughter, seemed just as eager to play chase as his own girls, her vibrant red hair bouncing out of the confines of her *kapp*.

Daniel couldn't help but grin as Rosemary ran, legs digging forward at breakneck speed, outrunning her elder sister as well as a girl five years her senior. The girl had wings. He no longer worried about her finding her footing, glad she and Hannah had finally knocked down their walls together. When Rosemary reached the fence lines, sliding to a stop in the damp grass, she smiled at him as if accomplishing a great feat. He smiled back. This was just another step of her feeling more alive, the little girl who sang and charmed bees, and felt loved.

"Girl can sure run," Joshua said, stepping out onto the porch.

"You should see Hannah run from a rooster. They come by it naturally," Daniel chuckled.

Joshua nursed a glass of tea, Hannah's well-brewed blend, and sat down beside him. "So, all this nonsense is done."

"*Jah*. They said there would be a court date, but they have enough on him that they don't need Rosemary. I wasn't going to let her testify anyhow." Neither Rosemary nor Catherine would ever see a monster's face again if he had any say in the matter.

"It isn't our way, *jah*. It wonders me what tomorrow may bring," Joshua said lightly as he took a drink.

"Now, *Onkel*, you know that is for *Gott* alone to know." Daniel gave him a sideways smirk. Joshua was just prodding for information.

"*Ach*, boy, tell an old man. I like a happy story as much as the next one and Edith has been worried Hannah is going to up and take those *kinner* away. You know she thinks of them like her own."

"I'm working on that," Daniel replied. "I gave her flowers. Well, left them in her room for when she woke."

"In November?"

"We have a florist in town," Daniel laughed. "And?"

"House has been full of people since she woke. But I'm getting to it." He did note the flowers now sat in the center of the sitting room coffee table and her smile was much brighter today. For two days, they had barely spoken, neither of them knowing how to take the next step. Having three children underfoot and constant visitors about didn't help much either.

Hannah stepped outside and called everyone inside. She was wearing her chicory-blue dress, his favorite. He hoped it wasn't by accident.

After grace was said, and the meal was devoured, Hannah and the women begin clearing the table. Catherine gave him a sharp glare. Daniel leaned toward her. "I don't break promises, but you need some patience."

"I need you to make this a better day than it has been already. You promised last night you would talk to her today," Catherine urged. "Do you want us to leave?" Daniel stood, gave her a wink and made his way over to Hannah.

M.J. tugged at her apron and Hannah bent down to her. "What is it?" Her little girl bit her lip, looking almost worried.

"Is the bad man gone now?"

Hannah knelt and hugged her. "Oh, yes. He is gone. Everything is all right now. We are all safe."

"So we don't have to play pretend anymore," M.J. whispered loudly. Hannah jerked to attention, her eyes catching Millie's right away. Millie smiled, waved off the worry. No one would speak it out loud, but Hannah's coming here was no longer a secret. Daniel liked that, feeling no pressure to uphold so much.

"No, M.J.," Daniel spoke up. "No more pretending. Now help the ladies clean up and don't eat all that pie before we get back."

"Where are you going?"

"I'm going courting," Daniel said and watched Hannah's eyes widen. Giggles from the table made her cheeks rosier than the already hot kitchen had. "Come, Mrs. Raber." Daniel held out a hand and she shyly slipped her fingers into it.

"Where are we going?" she asked as he reached for her coat and shawl, helped her slip into them.

"Anywhere we want." He smiled down to her, relishing the soft features of her face, the look of affection in her eyes, and the excitement of anticipation.

The air was cold enough Hannah could see her own breath, but inside her heart was pounding enough that she figured if frostbite was a potential threat, she wouldn't notice. Sitting beside the man she loved, heading to an unknown destination without the need to glance over their shoulders.

"I had a talk with the girls. They don't want

to leave." Daniel veered Colt onto the main road and toward Millie's orchard.

"I know. They love it here."

"I'm sure Bates can help you start from anywhere, give you back some familiarities you have been without these few months."

"He could." But she didn't want that. How could she tell him what she truly wanted? Men like him required a strong, confident woman, and Hannah was neither.

"I have grown to love your *dochdern*." So he wasn't asking her to stay. Her heart plummeted. Daniel feared losing her daughters. Hannah felt the first tears touch her cold cheek as he veered off the gravel road and pulled into the orchard grass. The trees were dormant, barren, like her life right now felt. Cold and miserable and fruitless.

"I know you care about them. You are welcome to come see them anytime, but I can't stay and keep doing this, this pretend marriage." Daniel turned to face her. His hand reached up, brushed the tears from her cheek. "I already lived that, and I can't do it again. I just want to live a simple, quiet life with my children."

"If you want to go, I won't stop you, but…" His voice lowered, his warm fingers pressed closer against her flesh. "I want more."

"You want me to stay for them, for you to not lose them?"

"I want you to stay because I love you, Hannah. Stay because I can't imagine a life without you in it."

"Daniel, I know what the children mean to you…"

"No, Hannah," he stopped her. "I have struggled with this a while. What I feel for you. I tried not to. You were Michael's wife. How could I fall in love with you? How could I give you the life you were accustomed to? But I have to be honest, even that first night I saw you, I knew." He leaned in closer. "The girls were easy to love, you, my dear wife, were impossible not to."

"Do you really mean that, Daniel? You aren't just saying you are willing to keep me because of them?"

He leaned down and kissed her, soft and tenderly. "I love you because you are everything I searched for in a woman all my life but never found." His lips brushed hers once more. "I love you because you value everything that matters—God, family and community." He kissed her cheek. "I love you because I can't stand not to be near you. I can't imagine you not beside me when I wake, when I fall asleep. I can't not love you, Hannah Raber."

"I love you too, Daniel, but you have to be sure. I can't spend the rest of my life feeling like a bad choice or someone you will tire of. I can't stay just so in ten years you will be bored with me."

"How could I when I can't even get enough of you." His smile became another kiss, hopeful and sweet, an unspoken promise to years of happiness to come.

He pulled away slowly. "We can build a life here. Together." That's all she ever wanted.

"And add to it." She looked up with hopeful eyes and his heart wasn't sure it could take much more. "I love children," she admitted.

"I would love to have more children with you, Hannah Raber."

"*Ich liebe dich*, Daniel Raber."

"I love you too, Hannah Raber."

Throwing caution to the wind, Hannah rushed forward and kissed him again. Whatever came, he would always hold her up and she him.

* * * * *

If you enjoyed
His Amish Wife's Hidden Past,
look for these other emotionally gripping
and wonderful Amish stories

Snowbound with the Amish Bachelor
by Patricia Johns

An Unexpected Amish Harvest
by Carrie Lighte

The Cowboy's Amish Haven
by Pamela Desmond Wright

Available now from Love Inspired!

Find more great reads at
www.LoveInspired.com

Dear Reader,

Thank you for taking a trip with me to Miller's Creek, Kentucky. Though fictional, this community was built on the landscapes and wonderful people I have encountered in my life. There are many amazing things about the Amish that have inspired me, but with every book I've written, it is their strong sense of community that has inspired me most.

Daniel Raber will always be a favorite hero of mine. Mostly for the role he plays in the Raber girls' lives. Stepfathers are rarely acknowledged for the amazing men that they are.

Daniel and Hannah's story also reminds me that we cannot become prisoners of our past. None of us are perfect, nor has everyone been blessed with strong families. But God doesn't abandon. Even when we think we are lost and alone, He places us within communities, sometimes with strangers, to lift us up until the storms pass.

May we always continue to give God thanks for his many blessings and when we find ourselves in a place of contentment, may we always remember to help another.

Thank you for reading and I hope you can

stop in soon and visit me at mindysteeleauthor. wordpress.com, on Facebook @Mindy Steele Author, or Instagram@msteele07.

Blessings,
Mindy

HARLEQUIN SELECTS COLLECTION

**From Robyn Carr to RaeAnne Thayne to
Linda Lael Miller and Sherryl Woods we promise
(actually, GUARANTEE!) each author in the
Harlequin Selects collection has seen their name on
the *New York Times* or *USA TODAY* bestseller lists!**